THE LAIRD OF LOCHARRUN

When Gilbert Meredith jilted her all Lorna wanted was to get away as far from him as possible, so she jumped at the chance of going to Scotland to look after old Mrs Lamond. But what had Gilbert told the old lady's grandson, the formidable Craig Lamond, to make him so hostile to Lorna?

THE LAIRD OF LOCHARRUN

BY

ANNE HAMPSON

MILLS & BOON LIMITED
LONDON W1

First published 1980

Australian copyright 1980
Philippine copyright 1980
This edition 1980
© Anne Hampson 1980

ISBN 0 263 73289 4

Set in Linotype Times 11 on 11½ pt.

*Made and printed in Great Britain by
Richard Clay (The Chaucer Press), Ltd, Bungay, Suffolk*

CHAPTER ONE

LORNA WOODROW lowered her head as Nurse Symonds asked the question,

'Is something wrong? You look ready to burst into tears.'

'It's nothing.' Lorna spoke more abruptly than she intended, but she was desperately trying to keep the sob from her voice. 'I expect I'm tired.'

'Well, you'll be off duty in another half hour.' Eileen Symonds glanced at her watch. 'You've just time to tuck in your favourite patients and then you'll be away. Are you seeing Gilbert tonight——?' Eileen stopped and grimaced. 'I mean, of course, Dr Meredith,' she added. 'Lucky you, managing to win the most handsome and eligible doctor on the hospital staff! You do realise, I suppose, that every other nurse here envies you?'

Again Lorna avoided her colleague's eyes, and her lip quivered as she said,

'Please excuse me, Eileen. I really must hurry.'

Nurse Symonds frowned a little.

'Something *is* wrong, Lorna. Can't you tell me about it?'

Dumbly Lorna shook her head and walked away in the direction of the ward, tears gathering in her lovely hazel eyes. Yes, something was wrong, and very soon it would be no secret that the engagement between Dr Gilbert Meredith and Nurse Woodrow had been broken off.

Even now, eight hours after Gilbert had sent for her and almost callously broken the news that he no longer loved her, Lorna could not believe it had really happened. It was a bad dream from which she *must* awaken! Gilbert had adored her almost from the moment of his coming here to the Cardon General hospital. Nurses and doctors alike had noticed where his interest lay and it had been no surprise to anybody when the engagement was announced.

And now it was all over. Gilbert had met someone else.

'Ah, here you are Nurse, with my nightcap! I'm well aware that it isn't your duty to bring it to me, dear, but it never tastes the same when the night nurse makes it. I have an idea she adds a little water, instead of using all milk.' Mrs Kirkwood, an elderly patient, spoke quietly as Lorna came to her bedside with the tray. 'You look tired, and a little unhappy. You shouldn't—not at your age, and being engaged to that charming young doctor.'

Lorna managed a smile; she had persevered throughout the day to hide her agony of heart and mind, and she wondered just how she had produced her customary cheery smile which the patients expected of her.

'What a sunny disposition you have, Nurse,' was the comment often heard on the ward where she worked. 'You're the only tonic we need!'

At last Lorna was on her way home, to the house of her uncle and aunt, the couple who had willingly taken her when her parents had died within six months of one another, Lorna being only seventeen at the time. That was five years ago, and never for one moment had Lorna ceased to be grateful for the home, and the affection, that had been given so freely to her. On hearing of the broken engagement her aunt would comfort her as best she could, while her uncle would become furiously angry at the idea that any man could jilt his niece.

But they were out when Lorna arrived home; the house was in darkness, grim and forbidding to Lorna in her present state of mind. She felt lost, deserted, and although she fought the tears they fell abundantly as, having let herself in by the front door, she mounted the stairs without switching on a light.

She took off her coat and flung it over the back of a chair, then lay down on the bed, her heart breaking at the thought of Gilbert being with another girl this evening. It was Tuesday, and whenever possible they went out to a dinner dance which was held weekly at one of the big hotels in town. Lorna would wear a long dress and always her fiancé would say some word of flattery as his appreciative eyes swept over her slender figure.

'This particular dress enhances the tawny-gold of your hair,' he would tell her lovingly; or, 'You should wear white more often, my darling. It seems to accentuate the alabaster quality of your skin and that adorable, delicate peach-bloom of your cheeks.'

No more would she hear his flattery. That would now be given to another girl, the daughter of a wealthy businessman whose successes had been a feature of an article in the national press recently.

At length Lorna sat up on the bed and dried her tears. She supposed that one day—in the far future —she would be able to laugh again, that this hurt would have faded, and with it the memories which at the present time were so unbearably painful and persistent.

Where could her aunt and uncle have gone to? It was not often that they were out on her arrival home from the hospital. Sometimes they would decide to go to the cinema, or perhaps to visit one or other of their friends. But usually they would mention this so that Lorna would be prepared to find them out. She wanted them tonight of all nights. She desired the sympathy and the compassion which they would extend to her. She wanted a shoulder to cry upon, a soft and gentle voice to soothe her hurt.

She left the bed and went to the door, with the intention of going downstairs, but she stopped as she heard the key in the front door. The voices of her aunt and uncle could be heard, but there was another voice also, that of their friend Mrs Ashworth, who occasionally dropped in for a chat.

'I expect she's been in and gone out again,' Lorna's aunt was saying. 'She's engaged, as you know, and they usually go off to the Randolph on a Tuesday, to the dinner dance.'

The light was snapped on. Lorna stepped back from the door of her room, aware of an added depression sweeping over her because of the visitor. She could not now go down, as she had no wish to make explanations before Mrs Ashworth. Besides, the tears had left their mark upon her cheeks and eyes.

'I expect you were glad when she got engaged?' said Mrs Ashworth in her clear and carrying tone of voice.

'Very. As you know, Stephen and I have always been all in all to one another and that's why we decided not to have children. We felt we didn't have the desire to give them our time and affection. We took Lorna, of course, and it was a difficult decision. But she would have been all alone and we hadn't the heart to leave her to fend for herself. It was a sacrifice on our part, because of the way we feel about one another. Our freedom was gone, as we could no longer make a show of affection towards one another just whenever we wanted to. However, Lorna will soon be married and we shall be on our own again....'

The voice faded as its owner entered the living-room, followed by her husband and their visitor. Lorna, rooted to the floor, felt a terrible pain searing through her head. Could she possibly have heard aright? Was it true that her aunt and uncle had never really wanted her with them? She had known, of course, of the great love they had for one another. Her parents had often talked about it and as she grew up Lorna had come to consider it to be rather wonderful, and when she became engaged to Gilbert she had asked for nothing more than for them to remain as deeply in love as her aunt and uncle had done.

Her aunt's voice came up to her again, rather faintly this time, but clearly carrying for all that. 'We're hoping they won't dally too long with the wedding. In fact, we're willing to help with such things as furniture if need be, as all we want is to get back to where we were before we took Lorna in.'

'It must be marvellous to care in the way you do, Mary.'

'We were determined, when we married, that we'd never change in our attitudes towards one another, and we've managed to keep to that.' It was Lorna's uncle who spoke now, in that rather gruff voice which Lorna had come to find so very attractive. For it had never been raised once towards her either in anger or reproof. Neither had her aunt's, for that matter, and so it was natural that she had lived in a false paradise, assuming that she was loved and wanted by her aunt and uncle.

'How long do you suppose they'll wait?' Mrs Ashworth was asking.

'Lorna's terribly in love, so we're taking it for granted that she won't want to wait very long at all. Gilbert seems very eager, too, but he hasn't much money yet, so he might not be able to raise a deposit on a house.'

'We're going to suggest they get a rented flat to start with,' from Lorna's uncle after a small silence. 'We feel we've done more than our duty and have no compunction in wanting Lorna to go from here. It will be great to be on our honeymoon again!' Another small silence and then, 'Won't it, my lovely Mary?'

A laugh, shy and quiet. Lorna put her head in her hands and wept. Unwanted both by her fiancé and her aunt and uncle. What a change had occurred in her life within a matter of a few hours! This time last evening she was the happiest girl alive—loved by her relatives, adored by her handsome fiancé ... or so she believed. Yes, a false paradise indeed, since she had *not* been loved, had in fact even been resented, in a way, by her aunt and uncle.

She turned and went to the window, opening it to seek for air. What must she do? Her whole life had collapsed and she could not even think clearly. All that did seem clear was the fact that she was completely alone in the world, with no one—*no one*—caring what happened to her.

All was dark outside; it fitted so well with the blackness within her heart and the hopelessness of her situation. She had known that she would have to leave the hospital and get another job. Now she had to leave her home as well. . . .

'Nurse Woodrow, Dr Meredith wants you, immediately.' The message was brought to Lorna while she was serving the lunch to her patients. She said, in a stiff little voice,

'Tell him I'll be there in about ten minutes.'

'But——'

'Ten minutes—or perhaps a little longer.'

She knocked on his door just over fifteen minutes later, entering in response to his brusque,

'Come in.'

Pale but composed, she stood just inside the door, which she had closed behind her.

'You wanted me?' Her beautiful hazel eyes met his across the room. He glanced away as he spoke.

'I've something to ask of you, Lorna,' he said, and came straight to the point. 'I don't want everyone here to know about the broken engagement. I mentioned this yesterday, but didn't stress it.' Turning, he looked questioningly at her. 'You haven't said anything to anyone here yet?'

Lorna shook her head.

'No, not yet.' She paused, but Gilbert did not speak. 'They're bound to find out. In any case, I fail to see your reason for wanting it to be kept secret.'

'You'll probably despise me for what I'm about to

say. But I honestly can't face up to being branded a cad.'

Shocked by this admission, Lorna for one fleeting moment wondered if her hero were not so heroic after all. She had admired his manliness, had liked the rather stern way he had with her at times; she found a certain attractiveness in the brusque voice, the confident air of authority. These all spelled strength ... but what he had just said could only be termed a weakness of character. He had jilted her for another girl, and yet he lacked the courage to face up to any criticism which might come his way as a result of his action.

'I see. . . .' was all Lorna could think of saying.

'No one need know——'

'As I've just said, they're bound to find out.' She looked directly at him. 'Would you rather I said it was I who broke it off?' No mistaking the tone of voice; she had not tried to be anything other than cutting. He seemed to flinch as he replied,

'No, of course not, Lorna, so there's no need to adopt that manner. After all, it's better, surely, for us to discover the truth now than later——'

'The truth, Gilbert?' she broke in, her pallor extending even to her lips.

'That we don't—— He broke off as she would have interrupted even yet again, but raised a hand to silence her. 'That *I* don't love *you*,' he amended then, and it was Lorna's turn to flinch, with real pain. She looked into his handsome face and a spasm passed through her body. Her love for him had been deep —it still was deep—and she knew without any doubts whatsoever that it would be some considerable time before she was able to laugh again.

'How long do you think this can be kept secret?' she inquired at length.

'I don't know.' Gilbert was frowning slightly. 'I must keep in mind my promotion, and let nothing interfere with it.'

'Your promotion's more important than my feelings. I still believe you'd be most happy were I to let it be known that *I'd* changed *my* mind——'

'I've never suggested that people should be told that it was *you* who'd jilted *me*!' he snapped.

Tears came with a sudden rush to her eyes, but she held them back, although she knew there lingered a brightness which, at one time, would have brought an instant question to her fiancé's lips.

'Darling, what's the matter?'

Not now. Gilbert was too engrossed in his own problem even to notice.

'I'm leaving the hospital,' she told him quietly.

He merely nodded in a sort of absent-minded way.

'I thought you would,' he said.

'You'd like me to go away from here?' If he heard the bitterness edging her voice he chose to ignore it.

'I have an idea, Lorna, although it might not appeal to you, since I know just how devoted you are to your aunt and uncle.' He looked at her a little doubtfully. 'You'd not want to leave them, I suppose?'

Lorna averted her head, hiding the sudden pain that entered her eyes.

'Tell me about your idea,' she returned, bypassing his reference to her aunt and uncle.

'You remember old Mrs Lamond who was brought in here a couple of weeks ago? But you couldn't possibly forget her,' he went on before Lorna could speak. 'She took to you in the sort of way a mother takes to her daughter.'

Lorna flashed him a puzzled glance, vaguely thinking that he had not put his point very well. However, she merely said,

'Mrs Lamond's old enough to be my great-grandmother. She's eighty-four.'

'Her age is of no matter,' returned Gilbert with a hint of impatience. 'What I was getting at was this: she told me that if we hadn't been engaged to be married she'd have carried you off to her home in Scotland——'

'Carried me off?' interrupted Lorna with a frown. 'I don't understand?'

'She wanted a private nurse, it seems, and you would have suited her perfectly. In the few days she was in here she certainly acquired a deep affection for you.' Gilbert paused a moment and, watching his expression, Lorna knew for sure that he was keeping something from her, something of vital importance. 'Would you consider private nursing?' he asked. 'It would be far easier, and much more remunerative, than working here in the hospital.'

It would solve her immediate problems, thought Lorna, but in spite of this conclusion there was an emptiness within her. She would be away from every-she knew, living among strangers and in strange surroundings. Mrs Lamond, who had been brought in after having a slight heart attack while dining with friends at a London hotel, had talked to Lorna a great deal, and it had been clear from the start that she had developed a sincere liking for the 'pretty girl with the sunny smile' as she had first described the nurse who attended her. Lorna had learned that

Mrs Lamond lived in the Dower House which was situated on her grandson's estate, her grandson being Craig Lamond, Laird of Locharrun. She was in London visiting a few friends, and it was a trip she made about every six months or so. Her grandson had wanted her to reside at Locharrun Castle, but she preferred her independence and therefore had insisted on living in the Dower House.

'It's luxuriously extravagant of me to want to keep up my own establishment,' she had told Lorna with a twinkle of mischief in her pale grey eyes. 'My grandson, high-handed, domineering creature that he is, would have me coddled in his own comfortable home, but I like to boss my own servants about. I have seven,' she admitted with a self-deprecating little smile. 'Craig considers it an outrageous waste.'

Gilbert's quiet cough brought Lorna back to the present and she looked at him across the large, high-ceilinged room.

'I don't know what to do.' A quivering sigh escaped her even though she attempted to suppress it. 'For one thing, I don't much care for Mrs Lamond's grandson.'

'Craig?' Gilbert raised his eyebrows. 'He's a friend of mine, Lorna.'

'I know.' They had been at university together and had corresponded at intervals, keeping in touch with one another. They were both thirty years of age, both athletic, but while Craig Lamond was a very wealthy landowner Gilbert was merely the younger son of a struggling shopkeeper. Craig had been sent for immediately Mrs Lamond was brought in to the hospital; he had arrived within the shortest time possible. Lorna had met him twice and did not at all care for

what she saw. She disliked his arrogance and air of
superiority; he seemed cynical and on the rare occasions when he spoke to Lorna—once when he had
been introduced to her by Gilbert, and once at the
bedside of his grandmother—his manner had been
grimly condescending, his languid tone of voice
seeming to portray boredom, his long unsmiling
stare appearing to be far too critical and penetrating
for Lorna's comfort. She gained the impression that
the autocratic Laird of Locharrun considered her to
be most unsuitable as a wife for his friend who, one
day, would probably reach great heights in the medi-
cal world.

Other nurses at the hospital had found Craig
Lamond attractive, declaring him to be extraordi-
narily handsome, with his bronzed, angular features,
his very dark blue eyes and mid-brown hair which
swept back from a faintly-lined forehead in a natural
wave. Well over six feet in height, and carrying not
one ounce of excessive weight, he had an athletic
bearing and a sort of lordly gait which accentuated
that air of nobility which is an inherent attribute of
the Scottish aristocracy. Pride in his ancestry was
portrayed both in his manner and in his classical
features. Lorna recalled her comment after her first
meeting with him.

'He might be a friend of Gilbert's, but he's nothing like him at all. He might be a god, judging by his
air of superiority. It's heaven help the girl he marries,
for I'm sure she'll be totally subject to his will.' Lorna
had been talking to her aunt, who had laughed and
said that there were many women who would just
love being mastered by such a man.

'Are you considering my idea, Lorna?' Once again

her ex-fiancé's voice brought Lorna from her reflections. 'You'd have a good life, up there in that lovely house. There'd be no real work for you to do—merely having to be on hand if Mrs Lamond should take ill again.'

These words came to Lorna but did not really register. She was dwelling on what she had heard last evening, was telling herself that she had no alternative other than to take this post up in Scotland—if it was still available, that was. She mentioned this to Gilbert, who instantly assured her that the post was hers if she wanted it. How eager he was! The pain in Lorna's heart increased at the idea of his wanting her to go away, a long way from the hospital, and from him. He cared not a rap that she would be living on a remote estate, with wild moorlands and high mountains taking the place of the gay lights of London. There would be no love in her life, no warmth.

She thought again about the formidable Laird of Locharrun and wondered how often she would come into contact with him. From what she had gathered from his grandmother the Dower House was completely on its own, surrounded by its own private grounds. The castle was of course close by, but in all probability its occupant's time was almost always fully taken up in the running of the estate.

Lorna, looking at Gilbert, noticed the twitching of a muscle at the side of his mouth and realised just how deep his anxiety was. She also realised just what he had in mind.

'If I accept this post,' she said huskily, 'you'll let it be known, after a while, that the engagement's just well—fizzled out, as it were?'

His sudden flush confirmed her suspicions. Yes,

this was what he had in mind.

'It would be best for both of us, Lorna. Neither of us would then suffer any embarrassment.'

'You do realise that people are going to consider it very odd indeed that I'm willing to go away from you?'

'I'll explain that we're having to do this in order to get some money for a house. Private nursing's far better paid than this——' He spread a hand in a little gesture of disgust. 'I don't think anyone is going to question our action,' he ended, and although Lorna raised her eyebrows at the word, 'our', she allowed it to pass without comment.

'Your friend Mr Lamond is going to consider it very strange, surely?' she said after a pause.

'He'll be told the same as the rest.'

Lorna's eyes flickered as they looked into his.

'In that case, Mrs Lamond is going to conclude that I'm taking the post only as a temporary measure,' she pointed out. 'She'll probably not want me on those terms.'

As she spoke Lorna was watching Gilbert's expression and she once again had the impression that he was keeping something from her.

'I'll think of something,' was Gilbert's rather cryptic rejoinder. 'Don't worry, Lorna, I'll make things simple for you.'

'And for yourself at the same time,' Lorna could not help saying, all the bitterness within her heart revealed in her voice.

'I can understand how you feel,' he had the grace to own, speaking in a somewhat contrite tone of voice. 'Yet I know, deep down, that this is the right decision for me to make regarding my engagement to you. I've found I don't love you, and that Susan——'

'Please stop!' Lorna's hands were clenched so tightly that the nails of her fingers were cutting into her palms. 'How soon can I start this new job? I'll have to give in my notice here——'

'I can pull a few strings,' he interrupted. 'Don't worry about that aspect of it.' He paused a moment. 'Your aunt and uncle ... they'll have to be told the same story, won't they?'

White to the lips, Lorna stared at the man to whom she had given her heart. He was her first love, for she had never been one for going out with boy-friends. Always she had known the right one would come along; she had wanted to go to him pure in mind and body. Well, it was all over, and she felt at this moment that there would never be another love in her life. Gilbert, moving impatiently, was waiting for her to speak, to make some comment on what he had just said. She wondered what he would feel like were she to relate to him all she had overheard last evening. Would he care that her aunt and uncle did not want her—just as he himself did not want her? She had no intention of telling him what she had overheard, of course, since she had no desire that he should pity her. But would he pity her? Not only did he seem fully occupied with his own thoughts, but the expression on his face was one of hardness which almost amounted to sheer ruthlessness, and it seemed impossible that he had ever held her tenderly in his arms, had kissed her with ardour and love, had told her over and over again just how much she meant to him and how impatient he was to make her his wife.

'I'll manage to explain to my aunt and uncle,' she

said huskily at last. 'You have no need for anxiety about their reaction to my decision to move up to Scotland.'

She was ready to go within a fortnight, poignantly conscious of the fact that her relatives and her ex-fiancé would breathe sighs of relief at her departure, and that they would be far happier once she was no longer around. Gilbert wanted to say a last goodbye, a circumstance that surprised her, and yet she could not bring herself to refuse his request. They met in a little café close to the hospital, and as soon as she saw him walk in she felt that something was seriously wrong. But when she ventured a question she was told airily that there was nothing wrong at all.

They had a pot of tea and a plate of cakes; the situation was fraught with tension and Lorna knew the meeting was a mistake.

Eventually the last goodbye was said and they parted, on the steps of the little café where they had eaten together so many times before.

'Good luck in your new job, Lorna.' Gilbert extended a hand but, somehow, Lorna could not bear the thought of any physical contact with him, so she pretended not to notice the gesture. 'I expect Craig will write about you from time to time when he corresponds.'

She cared little whether the Laird of Locharrun did or did not mention her in his letters to his friend. She rather thought he would have no time for such irrelevances. She found herself murmuring 'goodbye' in response to Gilbert's quiet, 'So long, my dear. Have a good journey,' and then she was alone, walking away from the lights of the café, towards the place where she would catch her bus—the last bus she would take from here to the home of her aunt and uncle.

Early the following evening her uncle took her to the station, where she caught a train that would take her to Perth. After travelling all night she arrived with just enough time to have breakfast at the Station Hotel before boarding another train that would take her to Aberdeen. Here she was to be met and taken the rest of the way by car. She expected a chauffeur, so it was not a very pleasant surprise when she discovered she was to be driven by the aloof and lordly Craig Lamond who, immediately on seeing her, came forward and handled her luggage, putting it into the roomy boot of the massive white car which she soon learned was one of three cars which he owned. His grandmother owned a car but, Craig explained, it had been taken to the garage for a minor repair.

'Did you have a pleasant journey?' Craig's finely-timbred voice was cool in the extreme, while his manner itself was almost frigid. Vaguely Lorna sensed something more than mere dislike on this man's part: she felt he was secretly regarding her with actual disgust!

'Most pleasant, thank you,' she murmured in reply. 'The scenery's magnificent.'

'It's different from your London aspect.'

'Very.' A strange prickle was running along Lorna's spine, and into her thought stream came that odd conviction that Gilbert had been hiding something from her. Why should she be remembering that at a time like this—and for no apparent reason?

'We have a three-hour journey before us,' commented Craig. 'The roads are hilly and tortuous.'

'You live out in the wilds, I understand?'

He shrugged his broad shoulders.

'It'll seem wild to you, I expect.' A small pause and then, 'But it's what you wanted, isn't it?'

She frowned in puzzlement.

'I don't think I understand what you mean?' she said, and her companion slanted her a strange unfathomable glance.

'I believe you do, Miss Woodrow,' was all he said, and because she was feeling so small and inferior Lorna allowed this to pass, although of course it both mystified and troubled her.

The car had turned inland and was travelling in a north-westerly direction, into the high places where a mist could be seen in the far distance. A silence fell and remained, an uncomfortable silence as far as Lorna was concerned, as the man beside her seemed to become more austere and formidable with every moment that passed. She thought of all she had heard about the dour Scots, their insularity and their pride. But the Scots she had met in the course of her work had all been jolly, ready for a joke, even though that joke might be against themselves. Craig Lamond was very different. He was so remote, so coldly impersonal. She might not have been in the car at all, so little notice did he take of her! She was exceedingly puzzled by his manner, for although she would not have expected any actual show of friendliness towards her, she certainly would have expected him to make some sort of polite conversation as they rode along, making for the thickly-wooded hills, and the moorlands which lay on the other side of them. At last she herself decided to break the silence, commenting on the scenery, comparing it with the soft downlands of the south of England.

'It's altogether harsher up here,' he responded. 'In consequence life itself is harsher.' A strange inflection in his voice lingered in her subconscious as she said,

'I expect you're referring to the life out of doors?'

The faint curve that came to his lips was almost a sneer, and served to add to Lorna's puzzlement.

'*Your* life will be easy enough. My grandmother indulges in every luxury available to her and you'll be living the life of a lady.' Tight the voice now, and tinged with contempt. And his foot jabbed the accelerator, as if stimulated by his anger. Lorna, astounded by the content of his words, and the manner of their delivery, could only stare at his set profile for a long moment, unable to put any logic into what he had said. The unfriendliness was so apparent, the sneer in his tone distinct and pronounced, mingling with the contempt, and with the total lack of civility. It was very clear that he had no wish even to be polite with her, and it was natural that she should wonder at the reason for his adopting such an attitude towards her. And then, suddenly, Gilbert's words came back, words which at the time they were spoken, had not fully registered, Lorna's mind being on what she had overheard the previous evening. Now, however, Gilbert's words were vitally important.

'You'd have a good life, up there in that lovely house. There'd be no real work for you to do—merely having to be on hand if Mrs Lamond should take ill again.'

No real work.... Undoubtedly these words fitted well with those just uttered by Craig Lamond,

'... you'll be living the life of a lady.'

Yes, both statements fitted. Did they have anything to do with Lorna's impression that Gilbert had been keeping something of a vital importance from her? She had gained this impression at the time when Gilbert was asking her if she would consider accepting the post as private nurse to old Mrs Lamond.

Mrs Lamond kept no fewer than seven servants, one of whom was her personal maid. So there was no possible chance of her being neglected if she should happen to take ill. There would be plenty of people on hand; also, a message would be sent instantly to her grandson at the castle nearby. Why then did Mrs Lamond require a private nurse? Starkly the fact stood out that she, Lorna, would indeed be leading the life of a lady!

But why? What was the old woman's object in bringing her up here, to live in her luxurious home ... with no work to do?

Craig obviously despised Lorna for accepting the post, knowing there was no work entailed. Suddenly she wanted to explain, to tell him she had not realised this at the time she had decided to take the post. Instead she asked, driven by some force she could never have explained,

'Gilbert ... he told you why I took this post?' Just *what* had Gilbert said by way of explanation? she wondered. For obviously he had not intended to convey the impression that the post was merely a temporary one as far as Lorna was concerned.

'He did,' came Craig's abrupt reply. That was all. Lorna waited, half expectantly, for him to enlarge on this, but he drove on in complete silence, his profile rigid, his dark blue eyes unwavering as they stared at the road ahead.

Lorna, both mystified and troubled, sat back eventually and stared around her, taking in the rising mountains, misted and grim, the wide heather moors, grey beneath clouds heavy with rain. It was an awe-inspiring landscape, wild and lonely; it would, she decided, suit her mood, since there was no light in her life any more, no desire for gaiety and laughter, and the company of other young people.

After a long while her gaze came round again to her companion's set profile. She spoke, asking how far they had to go.

'Not too far now.' Craig turned his head. 'Do you want to stop for a drink?'

Lorna shook her head.

'Not particularly. I merely asked the question for something to say.'

'I'm afraid you will have to excuse my preoccupation, Miss Woodrow,' he said tersely. 'My present mood is definitely not a conversational one.'

She felt snubbed, and fell silent again in consequence. That there was some mystery appeared evident. Lorna knew for sure that Mrs Lamond had her own particular reason for wanting her to come up here and live in her home. She also knew that Craig despised her, Lorna, for accepting the post. What she did not know was that Gilbert had given Craig an altogether different explanation from that which she would have expected. In other words, Gilbert had not given his friend the same explanation he intended giving to his colleagues, but had told Craig that Lorna had thrown him over, tempted by the offer made to her by Mrs Lamond.

CHAPTER TWO

MRS LAMOND sat in a high-backed chair, her spectacles on the end of her long, hawk-like nose. She wore a dress of dark grey velvet, trimmed at the throat with fine lace, ruched and scalloped, and on her wrists were several bracelets of gold, one with a diamond and sapphire clasp. Diamonds glistened on her thin fingers, and dangled from her ears. She made a regal figure, thought Lorna as she stood for a space just inside the room, after entering and closing the door behind her. Yet there was a stern austerity about the old lady which always reminded Lorna of Craig. She was tough, this aristocratic scion of the Scottish nobility. There was determination in the set of the mouth, obstinacy in the flexed line of the jaw. Yes, it was easy to see the resemblance between her and her grandson.

'Ah, there you are, my dear.' A rather theatrical sweep of her hand indicated the old lady's desire that Lorna should sit down. 'How long have you been with me now?'

'A fortnight.' Lorna looked directly at her. 'And I've had nothing at all to do.'

The thin pale lips curved in a half smile.

'You would rather I be indisposed, so that you would be occupied in tending to my needs?'

'Of course not!' Already Lorna had learned that the 'dear old lady' she had met in the hospital was a very different person from the mistress of Locharrun

26

Lodge. This lady could be both biting and sarcastic, although with Lorna she was almost always charming and friendly. Lorna had especially noticed this whenever Craig was present. His grandmother would actually dote on Lorna, much to Lorna's embarrassment, since it brought to Craig's face either an expression of contempt or one of sardonic amusement. 'Naturally I don't want you to be ill.'

'But it's only when I'm ill that you'll be employed.' Lorna said, with another direct look,

'Are you ever ill, Mrs Lamond?'

The old lady gave a short laugh.

'Scarcely ever, my dear. That little attack I had when in London gave me a shock, I don't mind telling you. Until then I'd believed I was good for a century.'

'You probably still are.' Lorna moved on her chair, uncomfortable and uneasy, for she was determined to put some questions to her employer, and she feared she might be snubbed for her trouble. 'Tell me, Mrs Lamond, what was your reason for wanting me to come up here?' Did the woman give a slight start? Lorna could not be sure, since she was fully composed as she replied,

'After that attack I decided it would be wise for me to have a nurse living permanently in my house.'

Eyeing her with suspicion, Lorna pointed out that she had seven servants and therefore there was no possible danger of her remaining unattended, should she be taken ill at any time.

'Also,' added Lorna, 'your grandson is always within call.' Automatically her eyes wandered to the window, from where she could see the turrets of the castle rising behind a clump of ancient oak trees. Beyond the castle towered the mountains, their summits sharply outlined against a clear blue sky.

'I believe I told you that I prefer to be independent of my grandson. This establishment is completely separate from the castle; my grounds are also completely separate.' There was a sharpness in Mrs Lamond's voice, and an angry glint in her eyes. 'I am my own mistress, in spite of my grandson's attempts to domineer over me!'

Taken aback, Lorna remained silent, wondering about this situation into which she had been drawn both by the circumstances of her broken engagement and the desire of her relatives to have her out of their house. She felt more uneasy than ever, sensed a deep antagonism between Mrs Lamond and her grandson, knew that she herself was—in some way which she could not begin to understand—being used as a tool in the hands of her employer. She felt there was some scheme afoot, yet on the other hand she could not accept that an old lady of eighty-four would want to trouble herself with such things.

'I would still like to know why I'm here,' said Lorna, at last breaking into the silence where only the low and heavy ticking of a grandfather clock was heard. 'I think you'll admit that you didn't really want me as a nurse?'

'Most certainly I wanted you as a nurse,' argued the old lady forcefully. 'Haven't I just said so?' Lorna made no answer and after a space Mrs Lamond added, looking curiously at her, 'I should have thought, Lorna, that you'd enjoy this rest after the hard work you've been doing at the hospital.'

'I prefer to be employed. Besides, I don't care for the idea of accepting a salary which I haven't earned.'

'Most commendable, my dear, and it's a pity my grandson can't hear what you're saying.'

'I don't see that it has anything to do with Mr Lamond,' was Lorna's rather crisp rejoinder.

'It might alter his opinion of you.' The words were spoken quietly, as if the old lady were talking to herself. 'However,' she continued, 'as you say, this business has nothing to do with him.' Mrs Lamond paused a moment. 'If you really are unhappy with the situation as it is, then perhaps I shall employ you as my nurse-companion rather than merely my nurse.' She looked at Lorna from over her spectacles. 'How will that suit you?'

'I would still like to know your real reason for bringing me here, Mrs Lamond.' Quiet the tone, but insistent. Lorna saw her employer's eyes narrow, her mouth compress.

'I am not used to being questioned by my employees, Lorna,' she said curtly. 'Please me by accepting the situation I've offered you, and we shall get along like a house on fire. And now, my dear,' she went on, changing her tone to one of almost gentle persuasion, 'perhaps you'd be so obliging as to read to me. I find the newspaper print a bit small for me these days.'

'Very well,' submitted Lorna, aware that she had no alternative other than to remain here for the time being. If, later, she decided to leave and seek another post, it would be only after she had saved up some money with which she could provide herself with a home of some kind, for she would never return to the house of her aunt and uncle.

After reading for over an hour, Lorna realised that Mrs Lamond was asleep. Her head had fallen forward on to her chest; her hands were lightly clasped on her knees. Rising quietly, Lorna went from the room to seek Katie, Mrs Lamond's personal maid.

'If she's asleep then she must be left,' declared Katie. 'If she's wakened from a nap she's a real shrew! Not for an extra five pounds in my pay-packet would I waken her!'

Lorna frowned.

'She looks most uncomfortable. If we could put a pillow beneath her head——'

'You can if you like, miss! But don't blame me if she tears a strip off you!'

'She'll have a crick in her neck if she remains in that position for long.'

'Not Mrs Lamond! Never has anything go wrong with her muscles. Hard as iron, miss, as you'll soon discover!'

Taking the girl's advice, Lorna left her employer to have her sleep out in the chair. The sunshine outside was inviting and she sauntered about the grounds for a while, thinking of Gilbert one moment and the next moment remembering that she ought to write to her aunt and uncle. They had no idea that she had overheard their conversation with Mrs Ashworth, and so nothing of an unpleasant nature had occurred between them and their niece. Indeed, Lorna had no intention that it should; she still felt grateful for their generosity in taking her in after the deaths of her parents, and it was her intention to correspond in the way they would expect her to. Now and then she would pay them a visit, but she would make it brief. She recalled their reaction to her pronouncement that she was taking the post up in Scotland. What a good idea it was! Such a sensible view on both her part and Gilbert's. True, they would be parted for a time, but there was ample compensation in the knowledge that Lorna was earning so high a salary and so she would be able to save up for the deposit on a house.

This was the gist of what they had said to Lorna; there had been no word of regret that she was leaving them, no sadness when the actual moment of parting had arrived. It was a chastening thought, this being unwanted. Was she herself to blame? wondered Lorna. Was there something 'not nice' about her? Her mouth trembled and tears started to her eyes. She was not indulging in self-pity, but rather in self-criticism. There *must* be something wrong with her, she decided . . . but what?

The question being futile, since she could not answer it, Lorna attempted to put it from her and concentrate on something else. The castle seemed close now and she stopped to stare at the beauty of the mellowed structure. A typical medieval stronghold, it had magnificent architectural features which combined the characteristics of an ancient fortress with a modern palace of elegance and charm. The castle stood on a low rise, with a backdrop of mountains, while in the foreground, grazing quietly, could be seen a herd of roe deer, roaming an extensive region of the Great Park. Waterfowl swam placidly on a lake, in the middle of which was a fountain. Specimen trees, ancient and massive, dotted the smooth green lawns, and statuary lined the pathways. Away in the distance a long avenue of trees gave evidence of the splendour of the approach to the front of the castle, while at the far end of this avenue two mellowed stone lodges stood sentinel to the park.

A little sigh of appreciation rose to Lorna's lips. Such beauty had not come her way before, and despite her unhappiness she could not help but respond mentally to her surroundings. Here was peace, and the bounties of nature; here was the freedom to wander where she would, over the wild heather moors, along a shining river where salmon frequented the deep pools, through some tiny hamlet or along the banks of a mountain loch.

She strolled on, without realising that she had managed to leave the grounds of Locharrun Lodge and enter the private grounds of the castle itself. It was the sudden appearance of the forbidding owner that made her notice exactly where she was. A deep flush of embarrassment rose to her cheeks and she would have done anything to avoid a meeting with him. But it was too late; she stopped automatically on the edge of a large area of ornamental shrubs and waited for him to cover the short distance that separated them.

His eyebrows were lifted questioningly—and arrogantly, she thought, as he enquired with veiled sarcasm if she had lost her way.

'No—er—yes, as a matter of fact, I have,' she stammered. 'I didn't realise I'd left the grounds of my employer's house.'

'Your—employer?' with the same veiled sarcasm which, this time, made her bristle. 'You've been engaged in some employment, then?'

She lifted her chin, her colour deepening, but with anger more than embarrassment.

'Your grandmother has decided that I'm to be her companion,' she informed him stiffly. 'I've been reading to her.'

His dark eyes flickered strangely.

'She asked you to read to her?'

'Yes——' Lorna glanced swiftly at him. 'Her eye-sight——?'

'Is as——' He stopped abruptly seconds after the interruption and it was clear to Lorna that he had bitten back the rest of what he had intended to say. But she could have finished his sentence for him; he was going to inform her that his grandmother's eyesight was as good as his own. 'With the aid of her spectacles,' he would most probably have added. Why he had stopped was also plain. He had suddenly decided not to say anything against his grandmother; his pride would naturally jib at making derogatory comments to a mere servant. And that he regarded Lorna entirely in the light of a servant was an undoubted fact. His very manner was all the proof that was needed.

'I'm sorry I trespassed on your land,' said Lorna, breaking an uncomfortable silence. 'From what your grandmother explained I gathered that her grounds and yours were fenced off from one another.'

'For the most part they are,' he returned coldly. 'But you managed to find the one small place where a path goes through from here to the grounds of the Lodge.'

'I'll take more care next time,' she promised, musing on what the old lady had said about her independence of her grandson. Did it mean, then, that she would not ask for his help if ever she was taken ill? He had been sent for when she was in hospital, but Lorna now surmised that Gilbert had sent for him, acting without even consulting the old lady. Craig Lamond had responded very promptly to the summons, so it was reasonable to assume that he had been anxious about his grandmother. The mystery of the relationship between the two was to occupy a considerable amount of Lorna's time, but for the present she dismissed it, mainly because Craig was speaking again, his austere voice breaking into her reflections.

'I expect you're now settled in? I hear you've been given the lilac suite.' His countenance was harsh and dark, his eyes narrowed and flecked with ice. 'It's to be hoped that you're happy with the luxury provided.'

She looked up at him, nerves tingling.

'You know which accommodation I've been given?'

'My grandmother made sure I should know,' was his cryptic rejoinder. 'I expect the next thing will be that you're provided with a car, and probably a personal maid.' And on that he swung away and, staggered by his words, Lorna could only stand and stare at his tall figure as, with long graceful strides, he made for the Falconer's Tower, through which he entered the closer precincts of the castle.

She turned, slowly and automatically, her whole mind occupied with what he had said. A car and a personal maid.... It was absurd! What was the man talking about? And yet.... She *had* been given the lilac suite, and she knew it was no servant's quarters. On the contrary, the suite formed part of the private apartments which, surmised Lorna, had at one time been even grander than they were today. The staircase leading to them—and to several other suites— was magnificent, while the suite itself, consisting of bedroom, sitting-room, dressing and bathroom, was furnished in the most luxurious manner, with tapestries on the walls of the sitting-room and rich carpets on all the floors except that of the bathroom. This was wall-to-wall carpeted in the modern style, to match the modern bathroom suite, lilac in colour and with gold-plated taps and other fitments. The bedroom was a dream in lilac and gold; the bed was a four-poster draped with lilac curtains, hand-embroidered.

'It's rather grand for me,' had been Lorna's protesting comment when she was first shown the suite. But her employer pointed out that, as the suite was not being used, there was no sense in Lorna's objecting to occupy it. The argument being perfectly logical, Lorna had made no further protest. She was glad of the private sitting-room, and she would not have been human had she not appreciated the sheer luxury of the suite as a whole.

Now, however, she was feeling extremely perturbed. She had been imprudent, both in her acceptance of the post and in her willingness to occupy accommodation which was quite clearly not what would normally be given to an employee.

On her return to the Lodge she was met by Katie, whose eyes where bright with anger.

'She's in one of her foul moods,' she said with total lack of respect. 'I don't know why I stay here! I expect one day I shall lose my temper and walk out on her!'

'What's wrong? I mean, why is she is an unfriendly mood?'

'Unfriendly?' repeated Katie with a raising of her rather thick eyebrows. 'That's mild, miss! She's in one of her most aggressive moods.'

'There must be some reason?'

'Her granddaughter telephoned—and it wakened her because, as you know, there's a telephone in Mrs Lamond's boudoir.' Katie seemed to have changed the words she had originally meant to utter, and Lorna, curious for some reason she could not define, asked interestedly,

'Wasn't Mrs Lamond pleased to have a phone call from her granddaughter?'

Katie's eyebrows were raised a little higher. But it was an instinctive gesture rather than a deliberate one, and even before the girl spoke Lorna knew that she would not say what was in her mind. She would be guarded, just as she was a moment ago.

'Jeannie and her grandmother don't always agree, miss, and this happened to be one of those times when Mrs Lamond resented being disturbed anyway.'

'So she was not very pleasant to her granddaughter?'

'She was mighty unpleasant!'

'What's Jeannie like? Is she young?'

'Seventeen and three-quarters,' returned Katie precisely. 'And pretty as a picture. Dark curls and merry brown eyes—and a sweet nature to go with it! I'm often amazed that Jeannie can be so nice to her grandmother, but I expect she's thinking of the fortune that's at stake.'

Lorna was silent for a space, reluctant to put more questions, as it seemed all wrong to be discussing her employer. But she was still very curious, which was not unnatural, in the circumstances. She said quietly,

'Mrs Lamond has only the two grandchildren to

whom to leave her fortune?'

'That's right.' The girl hesitated, her manner guarded as before. 'She's a strange one, though, is Mrs Lamond. Likely to do anything, if people don't obey her orders.'

A small silence followed. Lorna's appetite for information had been whetted, but she controlled her desires.

'I'd better go and see what she's doing. Perhaps she'll want me to read to her again.'

CHAPTER THREE

OVER the heather-clad ridge above the treeline a
small herd of roe deer—a splendid buck with velvet-
covered antlers and three does with their young—
were grazing peacefully, watched by Lorna who,
having roamed the moors for an hour and a half, was
now sitting on a little granite boulder, taking a rest.
It was warm and sunny, with a clear blue sky and the
zephyr of a breeze blowing over from the loch. Lorna
had asked her employer if there was anything she
could do and had been told to take the afternoon off.
It was the third time in a week that Mrs Lamond
had told her to take time off, and although Lorna
was vexed at the idea of having nothing to do she
decided that to remain indoors on such a lovely day
would be silly. And so she had gone off to roam the
heather moors, crossing several little burns on the
way, either by quaint wooden bridges or by the step-
ping-stones which someone had conveniently placed
across the streams.

Her attention was suddenly arrested by the appearance of half a dozen of the vicious hooded crows who
began circling above the deer, intent on disturbing
their peace. The deer grazed disinterestedly and it
was plain that they were used to the harassing tactics
of these repulsive birds who, Lorna had learned,
would not hesitate to peck out the eyes of some young
animal, or even an older animal if it happened to be
ill and therefore helpless.

She continued to watch the antics of the birds, but eventually her thoughts strayed to other things. She wondered what Gilbert was doing at this time. Yesterday he had started a fortnight's leave; Lorna had arranged to have hers at the same time, so that they could look around for attractive items of furniture and other necessities for the home they were soon hoping to set up.

And now it was all over. He was probably spending his leave at the lovely mansion owned by Susan's father. And when he did set up house it would be in one provided by his future father-in-law, since it was unlikely that Susan's doting parents would allow her to live in the kind of home which Gilbert could at present provide. Later, no doubt, Gilbert would do great things, because he had both talent and ambition. Well, it would be Susan who would be sharing his success, and not the girl who, having no real interest in money, would have been more than satisfied if Gilbert had provided her with nothing more pretentious than a little cottage with a garden where their children could play in safety.

A deep sigh that was almost a sob escaped Lorna as she sat there in the sunshine. She was so restless, undecided about her future. She felt isolated from anyone who really cared ... in fact there was no one who really cared. A sudden emptiness within her was a vacuum of utter despair, and her immediate surroundings did nothing to help. Whereas a few moments ago she was able to appreciate the dreamy moorlands and wooded slopes, the ragged heights above the loch and the conifer woods alongside it, all was now lonely and stark, the mountains tormented by the relentless cutting of the burns, the moorlands a little frightening in their solitude, and even the deer were dark silhouettes merging with the sombre landscape.

Lorna shivered, and rose to her feet. What must she do? What was there for her now? She could not remotely envisage ever falling in love again, so she must try to form a plan for her future. She felt she would prefer to leave nursing, but what else was there for her to do? Another sigh and a switch of thoughts which was not intentional. She was troubled by the mystery that surrounded her presence here and for a space this occupied her mind to the exclusion of all else. Mrs Lamond had two sides to her nature, but with Lorna she was almost always gracious and smiling. However, Lorna had seen the other side of her on a couple of occasions and she definitely did not care for what she had witnessed. She could treat her servants like slaves, and Lorna had heard from Mrs Hailsham, the housekeeper, that it was only the idea that they would be left legacies that kept Mrs Lamond's servants with her.

Lorna wondered if they were cherishing false hopes, as she could well imagine the old lady leaving them nothing at all.

It was a week since Katie's words, arousing Lorna's curiosity as to the relationship existing between Mrs Lamond and her granddaughter, had been uttered.

'She's a strange one, though, is Mrs Lamond. Likely to do anything, if people don't obey her orders.'

Yes, a strange one indeed, thought Lorna, beginning to retrace her steps along the narrow path that had been cut through the moors by Craig's gamekeepers and others in his employ. The old lady was deep, too, and she was using Lorna—or intending to use her—in some scheme which, she had already surmised, had been guessed at by her grandson. This would account for his dislike of Lorna, who had reached this conclusion only after spending some considerable time in trying to explain this dislike, and the contempt that had accompanied it whenever he happened to be in her company. She had come face to face with him the previous afternoon when, after being closeted with his grandmother in her boudoir for over an hour, he had emerged to find Lorna in the hall, arranging flowers in a huge copper urn standing between two shining suits of armour. She had straightened up involuntarily; it was a dark harsh countenance she saw which fleetingly brought visions of bygone days of savage tribal warfare with proud chiefs engaging their men in lawless, bloodthirsty deeds. It was plain to Lorna that the interview with his grandmother had left Craig furiously angry.

He stood for a moment, his contemptuous eyes roving her slender figure in such a way that Lorna, hot with embarrassment, tilted her chin, a question in the sparkle that entered her eyes.

'Mind you don't overtax yourself,' he sneered and, without waiting to see if she could find a retort, the arrogant laird of Locharrun strode the length of the hall to the massive oak door. Fury burned within Lorna and for one impulsive moment she knew the urge to run after him and demand an explanation for his words. The conviction that he would only snub her further caused her to hesitate, but there was a determined element about her as she bent to resume her task. Somehow she was going to solve the mystery of her presence in this house ... somehow, but when, and where, would the opportunity arise?

Now, as she wandered back over the moors, Lorna was half-inclined to abandon the attempt and instead to give in her notice right away. She felt the presence of some evil, of some devilment in the attitude of the old lady who, at first, when she had seen her in the London hospital, had seemed so charming and affable. She had taken a strong liking to Lorna, as Gilbert had said, and it was a fact that Lorna liked her in return. She had given no trouble, had never grumbled about food or attention as many old people were so often doing. In fact she had been a model patient and the nurses had all declared that it would have been a pleasure to have gone on looking after her.

The idea of handing in her notice was soon thrust aside as the exigency of her situation was borne upon her. True, she had savings—money, she recalled with a little silent sob, that had been put aside for the home she would make with Gilbert—but they would not last long. She had to find a home, then furnish it. Where would this home be? Not in Scotland, naturally, since there was no reason at all why she should settle here. Yet if she went back to London her aunt and uncle would have to be told that the engagement was broken. They would have to know eventually, but for some reason she could not explain Lorna wanted to put it off for as long as she could.

'I shall have to remain here,' she was murmuring to herself as she entered the long beech avenue leading to the imposing front entrance of Locharrun Lodge. 'Yes, until I have more money saved, and by that time my mind will probably be more clear and I shall be able to make plans for my future.'

The following day she was in the village shop buying notepaper and envelopes, and looking for two novels which had been recommended to her by a colleague at the hospital a week or so before she left. Only one of the books was there and this, along with the writing materials, was in the hands of the assistant when a young man walked in, glanced at Lorna with a hint of curiosity, then went over to a revolving stand and began perusing the paperback books displayed there.

'Have you any less?' the assistant enquired of Lorna, adding apologetically that she had been short of change all the morning.

'I'm sorry, I haven't.' Nevertheless Lorna began searching at the bottom of her shoulder bag, just in case she had allowed some coins to drop down there. She shook her head. 'No, I've only the note, I'm afraid.'

'I happen to have some change I want to get rid of.' The young man came forward, holding out a handful of coins. 'It'll make my pocket lighter.' His smile was infectious and both the assistant and Lorna returned it. 'There, how's that?' He dropped the silver on to the counter and left the assistant to count it, turning his attention to Lorna. His look of appraisal took in the lovely colour of her eyes with their sweeping lashes, thick and curling. The peach glow of her skin had already been darkened to an even more attractive hue by the sun and by the fresh air which Lorna had been having in rather large doses since coming up to Scotland; her tawny-gold hair had, on the other hand, been slightly bleached, so its colour too, was enhanced. The young man's eyes even took in the crisp cotton dress and the light blue cardigan worn over it, the shoulder bag swinging at her side, the dainty strapped sandals revealing pink toenails.

Lorna opened her bag, aware that the young man's attention was still upon her. She fumbled with the second little parcel, dropping it to the floor. It was the novel which the assistant had wrapped up; the young man stooped to retrieve it, handing it to Lorna.

'Thank you.' She saw the smile, the frank blue eyes, the wide generous mouth, the rugged aspect of his cheeks. His hair was light brown, his eyebrows rather bushy and well marked beneath a high intelligent forehead.

'You here on holiday?' he asked, obviously having forgotten about the books at which he had been looking.

'No, I work up at Locharrun Lodge.' Lorna smiled again and turned away, leaving him in the shop. Ten minutes later she was strolling along the main street when she saw him coming towards her from the opposite direction. They both stopped, and it did not seem at all strange that he told her his name even before any other word was spoken.

'My name's Jeff—Jeff Townsley. I'm on holiday here.'

'I'm Lorna Woodrow.' She paused as if undecided about moving on. But it would have been so awkward, she thought, after their giving each other their names like that. 'Where are you staying?' Automatically she glanced around, reminding him that there were no hotels anywhere about these lonely moorlands.

'With my sister Gwen. She's married to a Scot, Iain Macrae. He has a small farm on Craig Lamond's estate.'

'There are about twenty farms, I'm told?'

'That's right—they're all rented to people like my brother-in-law. These farms are in addition to the vast home farm, of course. The laird keeps over two thousand head of Highland cattle, my brother-in-law tells me.' Jeff looked a little uncertainly at her before adding, 'There's a select little café just around that corner——' He flung out a hand to indicate the corner he meant. 'I'm just going for a cup of tea ...?' The unspoken question was not answered immediately, but realising that she would enjoy a cup of tea Lorna said she knew the café and had been there before. 'They have delicious home-made cakes,' she added with a smile.

They walked together along the street where the little shops, which had clearly been cottage dwellings at one time, were gay with coloured sunblinds and concrete tubs spilling bright orange nasturtiums, forget-me-nots, variegated ivies and other decorative plants. Reaching the café they went inside and were given a table by the window. Few other people were there, as it was rather early for the delicious afternoon teas for which the café had become famed among the locals and those people who regularly passed through the village on their way to the town of Aberfeldy.

'So you work up at the Dower House,' said Jeff thoughtfully when their order had been given. 'In what capacity?'

'I came as a resident nurse, but I'm Mrs Lamond's companion as well.' Lorna felt a fraud, talking as though she were really in employment.

'So you're a nurse? My sister was before her marriage.'

'How long are you here for?' enquired Lorna, changing the subject rather abruptly because she had no wish to be asked any more questions about her employment with Mrs Lamond.

'Three weeks. I'm employed as bailiff on the estate of the Flavells who have a castle just outside Alnwick. I expect you know of it?' Jeff leant back in his chair, his appreciative eyes fixed on Lorna's face. She saw his glance move from her hair to her eyes and then to her mouth. He was having a good look, she thought, but felt no resentment over it, and wondered why.

'I've heard of it. It's open to the public, I think?'

Jeff nodded.

'Every Wednesday and Sunday—and all Bank Holidays, of course.'

Lorna said nothing, her eyes wandering to the window and the garden where flower borders were so expertly tended that she was reminded of the superbly-kept gardens of the Dower House. A rustic seat was set beneath a spreading oak, and the shade seemed redolent of something not quite British in that it savoured of the exotic, probably because of the vine that had established itself among the branches of the tree.

'Here's our tea and cakes.' Jeff paid the waitress, shaking his head when Lorna brought out her purse. 'It's on me,' he said.

Lorna did not like the idea, but decided not to

create a situation that would probably be as embarrassing to her as it was to Jeff.

'Thank you,' she said simply, choosing a cream cake from the plate he held out to her. She poured the tea and for a few moments a silence fell between them.

'How long have you been up here?' asked Jeff after a while.

'A month, that's all.'

'I expect you love it up there, at that great house?'

'It's very nice, yes.'

'The old girl's a millionairess, so it's said.'

Lorna's eyes opened very wide. She had not thought that Mrs Lamond was as wealthy as that!

'A millionairess?' she gasped.

'Even wealthier than her grandson, and that's saying something. She inherited a fortune from her mother, and another from a maiden aunt—Dame something-or-other who owned a vast estate on the west of Scotland. She's been tight with her money, refusing to pass any of it on until she's dead.'

'It doesn't appear that her grandchildren need it,' commented Lorna, wondering just how much this young man knew about her employer.

'Craig doesn't, but Jeannie's not got much at all. Her mother married beneath her and they've been poor ever since. They live in that grey house standing on the rise just above the village.'

'That little hill to the west of here?' It wasn't a very nice house at all, Lorna had decided when she had first noticed it. Drab in colour, with small embrasured windows that seemed to give a grim aspect to the house, it stood starkly devoid of the natural embellishments provided by nature. Not one tree in the garden, not a flowering shrub or flower bed. 'How long have they lived there?'

'Not long. Their house was burned down about a year ago and they managed to get this one, but it's in a bad state of repair.'

Lorna, thoughtful, forgot that her tea was going cold. Intrigued as she was by the information being given to her, she forgot also that she had not wanted to talk about her employer.

'Surely Mrs Lamond could have provided them with something better than that,' she said, frowning.

'Undoubtedly she could, but as I've said, she's tight with her money.'

Lorna's frown deepened. Mrs Lamond certainly was not tight with her money where she was concerned; she paid her about three times as much as she would have earned elsewhere. The mystery was deepening, it seemed. Lorna wondered what would be the old lady's reaction if she, Lorna, were to refuse to take so much money from her, if she were to insist that her salary were reduced.

She said presently,

'Why doesn't Craig help his aunt and uncle?'

'I'm sure he would have done, but they're too proud. You see, Jeannie's father and mother are not closely related to Craig at all because Mrs Lamond married twice, having Craig's father by her first husband and Jeannie's mother by her second. When Jeannie's mother married a farm hand Mrs Lamond cut her adrift for years and then, about a couple of years ago, she began taking an interest in Jeannie, and it's thought that she's now made half of her fortune over to her and the other half to Craig.'

Lorna said guardedly,

'You seem to know a great deal about the family.'

'I've heard it all from Iain. He's lived on the Loch-arrun estate all his life, and his father before him.'

'It seems all wrong,' mused Lorna after a pause, 'that Mrs Lamond doesn't help Jeannie's people. What's the use of all that wealth if you can't make people happy with it?' She was frowning heavily, still not satisfied that the insufferable laird of Loch-arrun could not assist if he genuinely wanted to do so.

'It is all wrong,' agreed Jeff heartily. 'But with a hard, inflexible woman like that one can expect any-thing——' He stopped, a question in his eyes, and a hint of apology. 'Your employer ... you don't mind my talking about her like this, apparently?'

A slight flush rose to tint Lorna's cheeks.

'I'm talking about her myself,' she pointed out. 'I suppose it's not right for us to discuss her, but——' It was Lorna's turn to break off, yet in a second or two she was speaking again, admitting that her em-ployer puzzled her in many ways and that she was anxious to clear up a mystery which was troubling her. Jeff naturally asked about this mystery, but Lorna, glancing at her watch, gave a startled excla-mation and said she would have to be going. Mrs Lamond had told her she would expect her to read to her between four o'clock and half-past.

'Will you meet me again?' Jeff wanted to know, his manner eager and persuasive.

'Yes,' replied Lorna at once. 'Shall we say here, at about three o'clock tomorrow afternoon?'

'Fine! I'll look forward to that.'

It was only as she walked away that Lorna realised just how eager she herself had been in arranging another meeting between them. It was understandable, she was soon admitting; alone here, without a friend, she had quite naturally grasped the opportunity of another meeting with Jeff. He *wanted* to meet her and his eagerness was balm to the desolation that still dragged at her heart.

Immediately on entering the hall of the Lodge she was met by Katie, whose expression at once told Lorna that she had some important news to impart.

'Mrs. Lamond's lawyer has just left——' Kate glanced around; she was more than a little scared of the housekeeper and her sharp-edged reprimands. 'Altered her will, I shouldn't wonder!'

Something ran along Lorna's spine, cold and prickling. The unfamiliar sensation of dramatic suspense was like a file on her nerves. Why should Mrs Lamond decide to change her will—and at this particular time? The mystery seemed all the while to be deepening, and there seemed to be no way by which any enlightenment could be gained. A sudden doubt came to her: Katie could be wrong in her conclusion that the will had been changed.

She said, staring at the woman,

'What makes you suppose Mrs Lamond's changed her will?'

'Something I heard her say on the phone a couple of days ago. She was talking to Mr Craig, and she said, very forcefully in that way she has, "So you have only yourselves to blame! You've refused to do as I say and now you'll get nothing!" She was in a rare state, but only for a few minutes,' continued Katie, once again glancing around. 'After that she was all calm and composed, and she was smiling to herself as if she'd done something clever——' A cut in her words and a pause. 'I must go! Mrs Hailsham calls the old girl enough herself, but she tells us off if we so much as say one word against her.'

Lorna stood and watched her go, along the length of the hall to where several doors led off to various parts of the mansion. Katie disappeared, but Lorna remained where she was, nerves tingling, a troubled frown creasing her forehead. Some instinct, deep and strong, urged her to go right in to Mrs Lamond and give in her notice. Yet on considering this objectively she owned that it was not at all logical. For one thing, she had no valid reason for giving in her notice. For another thing, the alteration of her employer's will was no concern of hers. With a sigh that was a mingling of impatience and perplexity, Lorna went across the hall and knocked gently on the old lady's door.

'Come in, my dear.'

Pushing the heavy door inwards, Lorna went in. Mrs Lamond was in her chair, a book open on her lap. She had changed since Lorna was with her last and she now wore a most expensive fine woollen dress in navy blue. The buttons looked suspiciously like gold, so much so that Lorna was impelled to remark on them.

'Yes, they're gold—they've a safety-chain attached to each one and this goes inside whatever garment I have them on.' A strange pause as the deep-set eyes studied Lorna for a long, profound moment. 'You like them?' came the softly-spoken question at last.

'They're beautiful! I've never seen gold buttons before.'

'I shall make you a present of them, my dear——' An imperative hand was raised as Lorna opened her mouth to refuse the proffered gift. 'I want to give them to you, Lorna, so please don't argue with me!'

It was the sharpest tone the old woman had ever used to Lorna and its rasping quality made her frown. Very firmly she said,

'I'm sorry, Mrs Lamond, but I can't accept such a valuable gift. There are eight buttons——'

'Rubbish! Of course you'll accept my gift! Now, please let's have no more argument! Read to me—sit there, where I can see you full-faced.'

'Mrs Lamond,' began Lorna, 'I have no intention of taking those buttons from you.'

For a moment there was silence in the room, with only the slow, dull ticking of the antique clock to filter through it. Lorna stood in the middle of the floor, her face pale but composed. Mrs Lamond, on the other hand, was flushed with anger, and her mouth was tight. Her body was erect, giving the impression of dauntless will and powerful physical strength. Her words came slowly, almost menacingly,

'You will do as I say.'

Lorna swallowed hard, anger rising to cause a blockage in her throat. How dared the woman speak to her like that! She would leave her employ—at once!

But instantly the consequences of so impulsive a decision was brought into her vision. Where would she go? A hotel was of course the answer, but this immediately presented another question: how long would her savings last if she were forced to stay in an hotel for any length of time? She had spent so much on things for the home which she and Gilbert were intending to have, and all these items were stored at her aunt's house. They could be sold, but would realise nothing like the price originally paid for them. Besides, she could not write and ask her aunt to sell them for her. Such an action would lead to questions Lorna was not yet in the right frame of mind to answer.

The old woman was speaking, ordering her to sit down and read to her. Lorna obeyed, taking the book from her employer's outstretched hand. She noticed the prominent knuckle bones, gleaming through the parched transparency of the skin; she saw the fingernails, beautifully manicured; but nothing could hide the horny appearance which the years had produced. The wrist was thin, adorned with three bracelets of gold, one with a diamond clasp, another set with sapphires. A wedding-ring, wide and weighty; with a sort of nausea Lorna realised that it would never slide over the knuckle—if it came off at all it would have to be cut from the finger.

Silently she sat down and dropped her eyes to the printed page before her. She began to read, without absorbing a word. She suddenly hated Gilbert for the position she was in. Obstacles like unscalable mountains rose up before her as she tried to work out the best way of extricating herself from this situation. There was one way, the simple way. She could ask her aunt and uncle if she could return, just for a short time until she established herself in a home and a job. This idea was dismissed immediately in favour of one more acceptable. She would stay here for at least the next few weeks. She would take the sensible course and pander to the old woman, appearing docile and tractable while in reality looking around for another job. She might get one where she could live in. If not, there was always the possibility of finding a flat. She had not looked for one, so she did not know what might be available once she did begin to look. Perhaps Jeff could help her. At least he could get some information as regards the possibility of a domestic post.

'There's no expression in your voice, Lorna!' Mrs Lamond's words cut into Lorna's thoughts and she looked up from the book.

'I'm sorry, I was thinking of something else.'

'What, for instance?'

'It's not important, Mrs Lamond.'

'You're a strange girl, Lorna. You're close. I hate people who hide their feelings all the time.'

Lorna hesitated, but the words hovering on her lips just had to be voiced.

'Don't you hide yours, Mrs Lamond?'

The piercing blue eyes glittered, like lazulite; the parched mouth became no more than a thin cruel line in a sunken jaw.

'I'm your employer; my ways and my actions are not to be questioned by servants.' So soft the tone but with an underlying inflection that was almost guttural. Lorna shivered inwardly, and was more determined than ever to leave the woman's employ just as soon as it was possible to do so.

It was five o'clock by the time Lorna came out of Mrs Lamond's room; she wandered out into the grounds, lingering for a time in admiration of the various aristocratic features designed in the distant past by gardeners of distinction and fame. The terraces, which swung round in a half-circle and descended gradually from the magnificent entrance to the beautiful lake with its two bronze Pegasi guarding the flight of marble steps leading from the lowest terrace to the shore of the lake; the sunken rose gardens with their winding paths and grassy walks and tiny waterfalls tumbling down into the sparkling stream; the shrubbery with its blaze of colour created by azaleas, magnolias, rhododendrons and numerous other ornamental bushes and small trees. There was a Japanese garden—with brightly-painted bridges and little pagodas. It was surely made for children, thought Lorna, at the same time wondering what the gardens of the castle must be like. These were nothing in comparison, she had heard from Katie.

Lorna strolled on, reaching the avenue of massive beech trees, and then the Heron Gate, beautifully designed in wrought iron and originally forming the entrance to a palace in Venice. On reaching the road she stood, undecided about which way to go. She swung round, taking in the views of wild country, stark and severe. In a valley far below a chattering burn meandered through its deep defile—a gash in the basalt made through countless ages of relentless denudation. Beyond lay the wild moorlands, then the brooding immensity of darkened hills. There was a grandeur and serenity about the entire aspect despite its austerity. It was a place of legend and romance, of mystery and deep dark secrets. To Lorna with her vivid imagination it was not difficult to visualise this wild domain being ravaged by warlike tribes whose semi-savage chieftains took a sadistic delight in robbery, rape and hideous torture.

And Craig Lamond was one of their descendants....

She moved at last, towards the road on which was situated the imposing entrance to the castle. The gates were open and one of the lodge-keepers was standing by a small, ancient car, chatting to its driver.

Lorna carried on, past the end of the drive. She had not gone very far when, hearing the car, she moved in to one side of the narrow road. The car slid to a standstill and a young girl of about eighteen years of age smiled through the open window and asked Lorna if she wanted a lift.

'No, thank you,' she returned graciously. 'I'm just out for a walk.'

The girl looked her up and down before allowing her gaze to rest on her face.

'You must be Miss Woodrow, Grandmother's nurse?'

'That's right.' Lorna smiled and added slowly, taking in the gleaming dark hair, the merry brown eyes, the clear youthful lines of the girl's features, 'You're Jeannie—er—Miss MacFarlane.'

'Delighted to meet you. I'll draw in and we can become acquainted.' She immediately pulled to the side of the lane, tucking the car into a small space between the trees. She slid out with the agility of a fawn, and gave Lorna another appraising look. 'You're pretty,' she said impulsively. 'How are you liking your job? Exacting, I expect.' A wry grimace added humour to the twinkle already in her eyes. 'Call me Jeannie, everyone does. What's your name?' She grinned and added, 'Craig says I jump about from one thing to another, and I'm afraid he's right —as always! Forgive me, but I'm scatterbrained, just as Craig maintains. I act first and think afterwards. It's a dreadful failing which gets me into loads of trouble, but I expect one day I shall improve!'

Lorna was already laughing. She had taken an instant liking to the girl and she wanted to know her better.

'I don't expect you really are scatterbrained,' she said. 'And don't worry too much about improving. It's so easy to become dull.' Like me, thought Lorna, recalling with a sigh how she used to be before Gilbert's change of heart had taken all the sunlight from her life.

'You're kind—much more understanding than Craig. He's forever finding fault with me——' She stopped and bit her lip, but there was laughter in her eyes as she went on, 'I'm giving you the impression that he's an ogre, aren't I?'

'Well. . . .'

'Being diplomatic? Your job calls for tact, I suppose. Craig isn't all that bad, just superior and stuffy. No one would ever believe he'd been young!'

'He's still young.'

'No! He's over thirty—a terrible age!'

Lorna laughed again.

'Thirty is the best age for a man,' she said.

'It's an age of maturity, of feeling you're weighed down with responsibilities. Craig worries too much,' Jeannie ended, her glance going to the turrets of the castle outlined against the sky. On a high hill behind them a herd of roe deer grazed languidly in the warmth from the sun. 'Tell me about yourself, Miss Woodrow—— Oh, I asked you your name. Can I drop the "Miss"? It's so stiff and distant.'

'Then just call me Lorna.'

'I like it. My mother had a friend called Lorna, but she died—the friend, not my mother.'

'You live in the grey house one can see from the other road, I believe?'

Jeannie nodded her dark head.

'It's not a very attractive house. No one would

think my relations lived in mansions such as these——' Jeannie spread a hand to indicate both the Castle and the Lodge. 'I expect you've already heard some of the gossip?'

'Gossip?' repeated Lorna guardedly.

'Katie talks a lot. It's a wonder she hasn't told you about my mother marrying beneath her.' For the first time the lightness was absent from Jeannie's manner. 'Father's an angel! I'd rather have him than all the money in the world!'

Lorna said nothing; she felt there was no appropriate response anyway, so she just waited for Jeannie to speak again.

'Grandmother cut my mother out of her life when she married my father, but we're very happy, so it doesn't really matter.'

'Money is not that important,' agreed Lorna, but her thoughts went again to Gilbert, to whom money did matter—so much so that he was willing to marry for it.

'That's what I say, but Mummy is always advising me to keep in with Grandmother, because she's begun to take an interest in me....' Jeannie tailed off, colouring slightly. 'You see what I mean about being scatterbrained, Lorna? Here I am, telling you all the family secrets, and it's not more than ten minutes since we met!'

'I shan't repeat anything you've told me, Jeannie.'

Jeannie looked at her a long while and said,

'No, I'm sure you can keep things to yourself. I can—sometimes—but——' The girl broke off, her mouth quivering.

'Yes?' Softly Lorna spoke, the one word forced from her because of the expression on Jeannie's sweet young face, an expression that was causing Lorna some concern. Why should she feel like this about the girl? As Jeannie had said, they'd met only ten minutes ago, and yet there was an unaccountable weight of anxiety settling upon Lorna which, surprisingly, she neither resented nor wished to ignore.

'It's—nothing. . . .'

'As I've just said, you can trust me, Jeannie.'

'I shall remember that.' The girl turned towards the car, and opened the door. 'I'll probably see you tomorrow afternoon. I'm paying a visit to Grandmother.'

'That'll be nice for her. What time will you be at the Lodge?'

'Around four. She'll have had her sleep by then.'

Lorna nodded, watching Jeannie ease herself into the driver's seat. Lorna closed the door and stood near for a space as Jeannie turned the ignition key and pressed the starter.

'I might see you tomorrow, then,' she smiled, stepping back so that Jeannie could move. 'I'm going out, but I should be back by about a quarter past four.'

'Cheerio for now!' Jeannie was all brightness again, her eyes twinkling, her mouth curved in a smile that bordered on laughter. 'I'm off to see Craig now. He'll greet me with a frown and make some scathing remark about my hair needing a comb through it and the car needing a clean, but underneath it all he loves me! 'Bye, till tomorrow!'

Lorna stood for a moment as the car shot forward. There was a reflective expression on her face and the hint of a troubled frown between her eyes. She was interested in the relationship existing between Craig and his cousin; she was also interested in what lay

behind Jeannie's apparent gaiety. For a brief moment
she had revealed a deep anxiety, revealed it by her
quivering mouth and the dark veil that had been
drawn over her laughing eyes. That Jeannie had some
kind of problem was evident to Lorna who, owing to
her profession, was naturally alert to changes of expression or manner such as she had witnessed just a
few minutes ago. Perhaps, thought Lorna as she
turned to stroll back the way she had come, Jeannie
would confide in Craig, who would then surely offer
the help that was needed.

CHAPTER FOUR

LORNA met Jeff as arranged and they went straight to the café. Jeff did not hesitate more than a few minutes after they were seated, at a table in a corner by the window where the view was to the kirk and an ancient village inn and, more picturesque than either of these—attractive as they both were—the village pond where several species of ducks and geese swam about among the reeds. Willow trees bent over the sides of the water, and beneath these a few people were sitting, one or two of them throwing titbits to the birds.

'You were going to tell me about this mystery that's bothering you, Lorna.' Jeff looked at her, a half-smile on his lips, as if in encouragement for her to speak. It was plain to her that he was faintly anxious in case she had had second thoughts about confiding in him, but, strangely, she had not. She just had to speak to someone, and the fact that she did not know Jeff very well seemed not to make the slightest difference to her desire to talk to him, and she supposed that at the back of her mind there lurked the hope that with his knowledge of what went on around here he might be able to help her solve the mystery.

And within the short space of their waiting to be served she had related almost the whole, telling him about Mrs Lamond's being brought into the hospital, then the appearance of her grandson, who happened to be a friend of her fiancé. She had gone on, swiftly, to outline all that had happened since, and the only interruption which her companion made was to say, looking at her with unconcealed admiration,

'I can't for the life of me imagine anyone jilting you, Lorna. This fellow must have been out of his mind, because I'm sure this other girl couldn't have been anything like you!'

Lorna merely shrugged and continued with her story. Jeff had frowned heavily when she mentioned her aunt and uncle, and their desire for her to leave their house. Lorna spoke, quietly, unemotionally, continuing as if it were a recital which she was bound to give. And when at length she stopped speaking and looked at Jeff across the small table, she felt as if a heavy weight had been lifted from her mind.

'I just had to tell someone,' she said apologetically when he did not speak. 'Thank you, Jeff, for listening—and I know I've no need to ask you not to mention any of it to anyone—not even your sister or her husband.'

'I shan't do that, Lorna. You can trust me implicitly.'

She had know it instinctively; otherwise she would never have confided in him.

'I don't want you to think badly of my aunt and uncle,' she begged. 'I'd not have mentioned them at all, but as I was telling you the whole story I could scarcely leave that bit out.'

He was nodding.

'I can see that,' he told her understandingly. 'No, I won't think badly of them. In any case, that part of the story's not really relevant, is it?'

'No——' Lorna broke off as the waitress appeared

with the tray and their order was put on the table before them. 'It's the mystery—the attitude of both Mrs Lamond and her grandson that puzzles me.'

'You say she's changed her will recently?'

'Katie seemed to think so. It sounds as if Mrs Lamond had made some sort of an ultimatum and that Craig had rejected it.'

'It was believed, locally, that the old girl had left everything between her two grandchildren.' A pause, a strange glance in Lorna's direction and then, reluctantly, 'Who would be her beneficiary—if her grandchildren have been cut off?'

Lorna shook her head, wondering at Jeff's tone of voice, and his expression as he looked at her across the table.

'I can't think. Has she any other relatives, Jeff?'

He nodded his head.

'Many—a woman of that age usually has. But there aren't any close relatives that I've heard of— other than her daughter, that is, Jeannie's mother.'

'Perhaps Mrs Lamond's left everything to her, then.' It occurred to Lorna that she was moving rather fast, assuming what might not have happened: the changing of the old lady's will. Katie was a gossip; even Jeannie knew that. And so she probably romanced as well, as most gossips did, inventing what had never occurred. But the lawyer *had* been with Mrs Lamond; Katie had not made that part up. Lorna spoke what was in her mind, saying that although the lawyer had visited Mrs Lamond, it did not mean that he had been consulted about a change of will.

'No, you could be right,' agreed Jeff at once, watching her pour the tea. 'I'll have a talk with Gwen tonight—subtly, of course,' he was swift to add as he noticed Lorna's expression. 'I'll try to find something out about the family. Iain's a mine of information, but I haven't been really interested before, so what he's told me hasn't seemed to be of much importance. However, as I said, I'll have a go at getting some information.' He paused as she pushed his cup and saucer towards him. 'There certainly is a mystery. The old woman's up to something, that's for sure, because as you've said, she didn't need to have you in the first place. It does seem that she's got you installed there at the Dower House for no other purpose than to annoy Craig.'

'But that doesn't make sense.'

'He is annoyed, though, from what you've said.'

'Exceedingly annoyed.'

'He can't even be civil to you?'

'No. His attitude's been one of antagonism right from the start.'

Jeff stirred his tea thoughtfully.

'I wonder what your ex-fiancé said by way of explanation for your leaving the hospital, and him.'

'Didn't I mention that Gilbert said he would give Craig the same explanation as he was giving everyone else?'

'Yes—I forgot. Yes, you did say that Gilbert was going to say that you'd taken the job in order to earn more and, as a result, save more for the deposit on a house.' Again he was thoughtful, his wide brow creased in a frown. 'I wonder if he did say that,' he murmured presently, almost to himself.

'What do you mean?' Lorna stared at him penetratingly. 'There was nothing else he could say.'

Jeff seemed not to be quite sure.

'By what you've said, this Gilbert seems the sort of bloke who'd put all the blame on someone else.'

'He wouldn't....' began Lorna, then trailed off, fully aware that Gilbert *would* put the blame on someone else ... put it on her....

'You're not sure?' Jeff looked at her as he reached over for a cake from the plate in the centre of the table. 'You must admit that it would explain, to some extent, Craig's attitude towards you. Just think: if Gilbert told him you'd jilted him, for the money offered by Mrs Lamond—which is very excellent money, you've said so yourself—then Craig would obviously dislike you; after all, Gilbert's his friend, remember.'

Lorna's eyes were perceptive; she was accepting Jeff's theory, simply because she had had the impression, at the time she was having that interview with Gilbert, that he was hiding something from her. Yes, she understood now: he was hiding the fact that he had meant to tell his friend that she, Lorna, had heartlessly jilted him, tempted by the money and the good life offered by Craig's grandmother.

'He's ... hateful!' she cried chokingly. 'How did I ever fall in love with him, or believe in his integrity?'

'Well, you've had a lucky escape, that's obvious,' stated Jeff emphatically. 'Just you concentrate on forgetting him; he wasn't worth it in the first place. This other girl's innocent of what she's in for—— Perhaps she'll find him out before it's too late.'

Lorna nodded automatically. And then, as a memory struck her,

'Gilbert was not himself when we parted finally.' After going on to tell Jeff about that final goodbye in the café she added thoughtfully, 'He seemed troubled and I asked him what was wrong, but he said there was nothing.' She paused a moment. 'Do you think his affair with Susan had already gone wrong?'

'Could have,' returned Jeff, but casually. 'No use dwelling on something we can't answer, though. This other business is what we want cleared up.'

She nodded, wondering for the first time how she had come to confide so much to a near stranger. Yet she had no regrets, for she still knew the relief of having shed a burden from her mind. She felt sure that Jeff would do all in his power to help her solve the mystery, and before she left him she remembered to ask if he knew of anyone who might employ her. After promising to make some enquiries, he reluctantly said goodbye to her, having walked with her up to the high, imposing gates of the house. His sister lived farther along the road and he turned after he had taken a few steps, to wave to her. And at that moment Craig passed in the big white car....

Jeannie was with her grandmother when Lorna entered the house. Katie was sharp with the latest news, and with the information that the old lady's voice had been peevish and impatient.

'Jeannie's marvellous,' added the maid. 'So patient with the old fiend, taking it all and saying very little. But her mother'll be furious if Mrs Lamond's changed her mind about leaving her half her fortune.'

'You seem convinced that Mrs Lamond has changed her will.' Lorna looked at her. 'She might not have done, you know.'

'Then why was the lawyer here?' Katie whispered, glancing around. 'It must have been to get Mrs

Lamond's instructions about a change in her will.'

At that moment the housekeeper arrived on the scene and Katie scuttled away, disappearing in the direction of Mrs Lamond's boudoir.

'What's she been gossiping about?' demanded Mrs Hailsham aggressively. 'It's not the thing, Miss Woodrow, for you to be encouraging her!'

'I wasn't——' Lorna stopped, colouring. 'It was nothing, Mrs Hailsham,' she said, and without giving her a chance of saying anything else she turned swiftly and went upstairs to her suite. She washed and changed before going down to her employer's room where, after knocking on the door, she was invited to come in. Katie was not there, but Jeannie was; she smiled at Lorna and did not appear in any way put out by the old woman's irascibility, no sign of which was apparent as Mrs Lamond flicked a hand, indicating that Lorna should sit down.

'Jeannie tells me you've already met,' said the old woman in her reserved, aristocratic voice.

'Yes, we have.' Lorna smiled again at Jeannie, noticing her dancing eyes, her unruly hair, her 'don't care' sort of manner. But beneath it all was that anxiety; Lorna sensed it, and a few minutes later, when they had both been ordered from the old lady's boudoir and were in the hall, Lorna could not help saying,

'Is something wrong, Jeannie?'

The younger girl looked at her speculatively for a long moment before replying.

'I think I can trust you, Lorna.'

'Indeed you can, Jeannie.'

'Let's go out into the garden. I don't care for talk-

ing here, or in any of the rooms, because of Katie—
she listens!'

'Would she go as far as that?'

'And further. Katie's got a disease—curiosity. It's
always got the better of her. Mrs Hailsham would
sack her if she had the authority to do so.'

They walked into the grounds and found a seat far
from the house, a seat beneath a tree, with other
trees and bushes around it. The fresh breeze blew
down from the mountains and whipped their hair;
each looked enchanting in a different way—Jeannie's
hair being so dark while Lorna's was fair.

Jeannie said impetuously once they were seated,

'Lorna, I'm in love!'

'Oh....' Lorna was at a loss, not having expected
to hear anything like that.

'With the son of one of Craig's tenants. Grandmother would be furious if she knew, and she'd cut
me off. You see, she wants me to——' Jeannie
stopped, appearing to have changed her mind about
what she was about to say. 'So I can't tell her about
my boy-friend, nor can I tell Mother, because she's
set her heart on my inheriting half of Grandmother's
fortune—it's a million, I believe.' So casually she
spoke about a million! Lorna saw at once that the
money meant nothing to her; but it meant everything
to her mother who, having been disinherited herself,
was naturally hopeful that her daughter would not be
deprived of what would have come to her. Lorna
thought of Mrs Lamond, who was eighty-two, but in
the best of health, apparently. True, she had had that
slight heart attack in London, but she had got over
it very well indeed.

'Does your cousin know you're in love with this

young man?' she enquired at length, and Jeannie said that she dared not tell him because he'd be so against it that he might give the young man's father notice to quit the farm.

'Could he do that?' frowned Lorna, strangely unable to see Craig acting so ruthlessly even if he could. Much as she disliked him she felt he would always be fair and just, especially where his tenants were concerned.

'He could, yes. However, it isn't important at present because we're keeping our engagement a secret——'

'You're engaged? You've actually said you'll marry this young man?'

'Of course. . . .' Jeannie's lip quivered; she looked very young and very forlorn. 'When shall we be able to marry, Lorna? What can we do?'

Lorna shook her head.

'Nothing for the present.' She thought of Katie's conviction that Mrs Lamond had changed her will and wondered if Jeannie was gaining anything by keeping her engagement a secret.

'Doug's so patient and understanding. He doesn't care a toss for Grandmother's money, but he does understand how Mother would feel if I went against Grandmother's wishes and married beneath me—as she would think of it—as my mother did.' A sparkle had entered Jeannie's eyes with these last words. 'Why do people in Grandmother's position always consider that most other people are beneath them? Surely it isn't money that makes people nice or nasty? Sometimes I feel that Craig's the same; he has much of Grandmother in him, although he'd hate to be told of it.'

'They don't get along, obviously?'

Jeannie shook her head.

'Always at loggerheads.' A thoughtful, frowning pause and then, 'There's something I can't understand between those two, Lorna,' she said at last with a little sigh that sounded like frustration. 'I've asked him, many a time, and he just tells me to mind my own business.'

Yes, mused Lorna, she could just imagine him doing that!

Jeannie said after a while,

'I'm glad I confided in you, Lorna. I feel I've got rid of a load off my mind.'

Lorna grimaced to herself. She had shed a burden by confiding in Jeff, and now here was Jeannie shedding her burden by confiding in her!

It was less than three hours later that Lorna was to come face to face with Craig. He was walking in his grounds when to her dismay Lorna once more took the wrong path and found herself on forbidden land —or what she had come to regard as forbidden land.

It was an hour to dinner-time and she had decided to take a short walk. She looked rather shamefaced on seeing him and swiftly murmured an apology for once again straying on to his land. She was about to turn back when he stopped her and she swung around again, staggered by the tone of his voice as much as the words themselves.

'Don't hurry away, Miss Woodrow. You haven't committed a crime.'

She stared for a long moment in silence, wondering what had happened to the contempt she had hitherto invariably found in his eyes.

'No ... not a crime,' she murmured, scarcely knowing what to say. 'But—but I ought not to have made the s-same mistake twice.'

His eyes strayed from her face to the tawny-golden halo of her hair, gleaming like a precious metal in the sun's long slanting rays. She wished his face would relax, so that she could read its expression. Was there admiration in his gaze? The very idea astounded her, but what astounded her even more was that she *wanted* to see admiration in his gaze! This was crazy, she was telling herself seconds later. She disliked him intensely, so why should she care whether he found her attractive or not?

'It happens to be easy to make the mistake,' he rejoined suavely at length. 'There's always been a way through from my grandmother's house to the castle.' He paused, but Lorna found nothing to say. She was tongue-tied, dazed by the change in his manner towards her. 'Would you care to look over some of the castle gardens?' he asked. 'They're rather beautiful at this time of the evening, when the sun's sinking.'

She stared at him again, this time with sudden suspicion. It was not natural that he could change in his attitude towards her like this and she wondered what his game was.

And yet at the same time she was admitting that, if he *was* changing his mind about her, it would be far more pleasant for them both. Pleasant to be friends ...? Again she was staggered by an idea that had somehow intruded into her mind. Involuntarily a smile fluttered to her lips and she found herself saying,

'Yes, that would be lovely. Your gardens look very attractive even from this distance.'

He was noting her smile, and the faint blush that

tinted her cheeks. Her head was tilted, her eyes looking right into his. Something fluttered close to her
heart, and her pulse had quickened. The very air
around her seemed heady all at once, intoxicatingly
pervasive and sense-stirring.

'Shall we walk, then?' invited Craig, and she fell
into step beside him, excited at the prospect of seeing
his beautiful grounds. They were walking on a narrow pathway running between trees which met over-
head, but immediately on coming out of this the
vista was of forest trees in random groups, and Craig
told her casually that there were some of the finest
trees in the country among them. The oaks were
massive, and very ancient. The view opened out as
they walked, with magnificent lawns sweeping away
towards a lake and a fountain on one side, and an
area of parkland on another. Hills swept down on the
eastern edge, and behind them rose the mountains,
high and gaunt, their summits and sides bruised by
the merciless forces of nature—wind and rain, frost
and snow. And against this backcloth there rose,
dramatically, the turreted castle, ancient and mellowed, its massive walls having withstood many a
siege in days long past. What a heritage! It was with
awe and wonderment that Lorna, stopping involuntarily, stared upwards, lost in the magic, almost un-
aware of Craig's presence. He watched her, an odd
expression in his eyes, and although he seemed to
want to speak he remained silent, as though her interest in his home was of the utmost importance to
him. At last she turned, a half-smile on her lips.

'It's beautiful—everything about it! The setting—
the castle, the gardens.... Oh, but you must be very
proud, Mr Lamond, to be the owner of this place!'

'One takes it all for granted, I'm afraid,' was his comment, spoken quietly and perhaps a trifle regretfully. 'Others see more in it than the people who have been born here.'

'You were born here?'

'Of course.'

'Your parents——' She broke off, afraid that he would consider it an impertinence for her to enquire about his parents. To her surprise he told her they had both died comparatively young, just ten years ago. 'So you were only twenty when you came into all this?'

'Twenty?' he frowned. 'How do you know that?'

She coloured a little.

'Jeannie told me you're thirty now.'

'Ah, yes, Jeannie. She's met you and likes you.'

'She seems to like me,' agreed Lorna. 'I certainly like her.'

'You do?' An odd unfathomable edge to his voice brought Lorna's eyes swiftly to his.

'Yes. You sound as if you doubt it?'

Craig gave a shrug and began to walk on again.

'Would you like to see a little of the inside of the castle?' he asked, and again she stared, bewildered by his offer. 'I can see you're interested in old buildings,' he added, seeing her expression, 'so I feel you will enjoy half an hour or so in my home.' So gracious his voice! So different his manner from what it had been before. Lorna felt she should have been suspicious still, but his charm was sweeping away all memory of his previous treatment of her.

And so it was during the next few days whenever they met—often—in the grounds. He had told her she must explore at will and she had eagerly taken advantage of the offer. He invariably happened to be about; they would meet, chat and stroll together. And then, one afternoon, he asked her to dine with him.

The invitation was not altogether unexpected, owing to the friendliness that had grown up between them. Lorna accepted, and wondered if she should tell her employer where she was going. She decided against it, but felt uneasy, convinced that the old lady would not approve of the friendship.

She met Jeff on the afternoon before she was to dine with Craig. Jeff frowned heavily when she told him and said outright that he did not trust Craig. Jeff had learned little more than he had already told Lorna, but one item of information had set her thinking. It seemed that Mrs Lamond had set her heart on a marriage between Jeannie and Craig.

'According to Iain,' Jeff had said, 'Craig's told her there's no hope of a marriage between them. It's rumoured that he's interested in someone else, a beauty whose father has the adjoining estate—on the other side of the river. She's abroad at present but is expected home in a month or so.'

Lorna was frowning inwardly, the thought of Craig's having a girl-friend hurting inexplicably. However, all she said was,

'Mrs Lamond can't dictate to people. She has no right to expect a marriage between Craig and Jeannie.'

'She's a reputation for dictatorship. Her servants hate her, almost. She can put on the charm, as she obviously did when she was in hospital, because you believed her to be a very nice old lady, didn't you?'

'We all did. She was never any trouble—not like some of the patients we used to get.'

'See what I mean about putting on the charm?

She's poison, though, underneath.' Jeff paused a moment, looking at her with a frowning expression. 'Are you really going to dine tonight with Craig?'

'Yes, of course.'

He gave a short sigh of impatience.

'After the way he's been with you you ought to be highly suspicious of him!'

'I must admit I was at first, but he's so charming with me now that I've forgotten all about it.'

'Then you're crazy—if you don't mind my saying so! I'd suspect him——'

'Of what?' she put in with interest.

'I don't know—can't put my finger on anything, but I'm sure he has some ulterior motive, Lorna.' His voice had lost its curt edge and was persuasively anxious. 'Surely it's struck you as very strange that his attitude should change like this?'

She said nothing, a little vexed with Jeff because he had aroused suspicions within her which she would rather not have experienced. She liked Craig, was attracted to him in a way she dared not think about too deeply. He seemed to like her; he had taken her into the castle several times and they had had drinks together. He had given her a lift into town one day and they had had lunch together in a top class restaurant. Not once had he made reference to her job or her employer; no sarcasm, no question as to why she should have so much time to herself.

That evening, just before she was due to get ready, her employer sent for her.

'She's in one of her moods,' warned Katie darkly. 'She's had a headache for the past hour and she won't take anything for it. She always says pain-killing pills are poison.'

Lorna went along to the pretty boudoir to find Mrs

Lamond leaning back in her chair, the gold buttons dangling—on their gold safety-chain—from her thin gnarled fingers.

'The present I promised you.' There was a challenging glint in her eye, a warning tightness about her mouth. Lorna, who had reached the conclusion that Mrs Lamond had either regretted the offer of the gift, or had forgotten all about it, was taken aback. She was also determined not to accept the buttons at any price.

'It's kind of you, Mrs Lamond,' she said coolly, 'but I can't accept a gift as valuable as that.'

'You will accept. I also have something else for you! I've decided to give you some of the family jewels.'

Lorna's eyes widened.

'No,' she stated firmly, 'you haven't, Mrs Lamond, because you haven't asked me if I'll accept them.'

'Are you mad, child?' demanded the old lady wrathfully. 'The jewellery's worth a fortune!'

'That's the reason I don't want it.'

'I've a good mind to dismiss you—I haven't ever had a servant who's gone against my wishes!'

'You've probably never had a servant who's been treated as your daughter,' retorted Lorna spiritedly. 'There's a lot I don't understand, Mrs Lamond! An employer doesn't make this kind of gift unless there's some motive. I'd like to know your motive?'

'Well, you won't! Here——' She threw the buttons across the room. 'Take them! Pick them up!'

Lorna stooped, picked up the buttons and placed them on a table.

'If there's nothing else, Mrs Lamond——'

'Take them,' snapped the old woman. 'I shall keep

you here until you do!'

'You'll——' Lorna stared in dismay, glancing swiftly at the clock. Already she would be late, owing to this delay on which she had not reckoned. She had promised to be at the castle by eight o'clock; it was now half-past seven.

'Yes,' returned Mrs Lamond grimly, 'I shall keep you here, in this room, until you've accepted the gift.' She leant back again, relaxing against the cushions.

'You're having your dinner in half an hour,' Lorna reminded her hopefully.

'I'll have it brought in here. You can sit and watch me eat it.'

'I don't think so. I'm going out this evening and already I'm late.'

'Going out? Where to?'

'That,' replied Lorna quietly, 'is my business.'

'Why, you impudent creature!' Mrs Lamond's face was crimson with temper. 'You're employed by me —and you happen to be on duty this evening! Get that!' A fist was brought down with violence on to the arm of the chair. 'I want you here with me, until I go to bed!'

Lorna looked at her, aware that she was on the point of giving in her notice. It was so hard not to do so, in the present circumstances. But she did manage to control the impulse. For one thing, it would be imprudent financially, and for another—which seemed far more important—she had no wish to cut herself off from Craig, which she would be sure to do if she left his grandmother's employ.

'I'm not on duty, Mrs Lamond,' she argued. 'You said my hours would be from nine till five——'

'They haven't been from nine to five, though!

You've had all day off for most of the time!'

'That isn't any fault of mine,' Lorna was swift to point out. 'I'm more than willing to be with you during those hours, but you won't have me—well, only for short periods, to read to you.'

A sigh issued from the thin parched lips.

'Are we quarrelling, Lorna?' she queried, a dramatic change in her voice. 'I think a great deal about you, child. And if I want to make you this gift why can't you accept it graciously?'

Lorna shook her head.

'It's too valuable, Mrs Lamond.'

'That's for me to say! I want you to have it and I *mean* you to have it!'

Lorna glanced again at the clock. Almost a quarter to eight.... If she accepted the gift and returned it in the morning.... It was specious, but Mrs Lamond deserved it!

'Very well,' she said presently, 'I'll accept it.'

'Good girl! Take those lovely buttons and let me see them on a dress—that turquoise blue one—it has six buttons on it. Take them off and replace them with six of these.'

With a sigh Lorna picked up the buttons, then turned to the door.

'I'll say goodnight, Mrs Lamond.'

'I asked where you were going?'

'I'm dining with a friend.'

'I didn't know you'd made any friends, apart from Jeannie, that is, and you're not dining with her. Her father can't earn enough to keep them properly, let alone entertain.'

Spiteful creature! Lorna was beginning actually to

hate her . . . just as the rest of her servants did, according to Jeff.

Jeff. . . .

'I have made a friend,' she said. 'A young man whose brother-in-law has one of your grandson's farms—Iain Macrae.'

'Gwen's brother, Jeff? I know of him. He comes over once a year in the summer, and on occasions for Christmas.' She looked at Lorna. 'He'll be going back shortly?'

'Yes. He came for three weeks.'

'I see. Well, have a nice evening.'

CHAPTER FIVE

It was a dismissal, which Lorna thankfully took advantage of, hurriedly making her departure from the room.

'What was she like?' Katie's voice came to her as she began to mount the stairs and she turned, irritated by the girl's curiosity.

'Her usual self,' she replied curtly, and left the girl standing there, a look of disappointment on her face.

Almost three-quarters of an hour later Lorna was making a breathless apology to her host.

'Mrs Lamond kept me,' she explained, handing Craig her cape and aware that his keen gaze had taken in her appearance—the dainty evening dress of flowered cotton, the shining hair, the glowing cheeks.

'She kept you?' He seemed surprised, and his expression was veiled as he added, the cloak having been thrown over his arm, 'I thought you were—er —off duty long before evening?'

Lorna flushed at the implication.

'I usually am.' She wanted to explain many things to him, to let him know that it was Gilbert who had broken the engagement, that she had not wanted to come up here, nor did she want all the luxury that was being bestowed upon her. But the time was not right, for she had no proof that he would be interested. He was pleasant to her these days, but that did not say that he wanted to learn that she was blameless in all that had occurred.

'What was wrong with Grandmother that she wanted you, so late in the day?'

'It was a—a matter on which we disagreed.' Lorna hoped that the faint aloofness in her manner would convey the fact that she did not want to pursue the subject. To her relief Craig changed the subject, saying he hoped she liked steak Wellington.

'Yes, I love it!'

'Good, because that's what my chef is providing for us this evening.' A small pause before he asked, 'Does Grandmother know you're dining with me?' and when she shook her head, 'No, I rather thought you wouldn't mention it to her.' Another pause. 'But there was no reason, you know, why you shouldn't have mentioned it to her.'

'I suppose not.' She watched him hand her cloak to a manservant who had appeared on the scene; she was then conducted into a drawing-room where aperitifs were served. Craig was in evening dress, a tall distinguished figure with all the confidence of the aristocrat. Lorna wondered how she came to be here, then thought about Gilbert, who had been here on visits several times before he and she got to know one another. Gilbert was, therefore, used to this kind of life. He would fit in very well with the kind of life he would be living as the husband of Susan, whose father was reputed to be a millionaire.

'May I say how charming you look, Lorna?' Craig's voice drifted into her reverie and a smile fluttered to her lips.

'Thank you, Craig.' It was still a matter of wonder to her that she and he were using Christian names, but he had insisted almost from that first day, when he had dropped his attitude of hostility and instead adopted this most attractive manner that was fast making her forget Gilbert and the hurt she had sustained at his hands.

Craig cast another appreciative glance in her direction.

'My grandmother always had a weakness for a pretty girl,' he said, sitting down with his drink and keeping his eyes upon her.

'Oh ... did she?'

'I've embarrassed you.' He gave a short, humourless laugh. 'Sorry, Lorna. I was thinking aloud.'

She looked hard at him, recalling both her own suspicions, and those of Jeff. Could Craig possibly have some ulterior motive in making up to her like this? Just now there had seemed to be a kind of mocking satire in his words, which was out of keeping with the friendliness he was always extending towards her these days.

They went from the drawing room to the dining room, a high-ceilinged apartment with an oriel window at one end and three huge bay windows along the south side. Fine old tapestries hung on the walls. The furniture was French, the silver on the table Georgian. Lorna had seen luxury and good taste at the house of her employer, but this even exceeded it. She fell to thinking about the girl Craig would one day marry, who would become mistress of all this.

He drew out her chair for her; she noticed that the table had been made smaller by the withdrawal of leaves and was grateful to Craig for his thoughtfulness, since she would have felt most awkward if she had been forced to sit at a massive table, trying to converse with her host across a great distance. It was a cosy meal, served by the butler and a younger manservant. Wine accompanied every course and when the meal was finished they went to the drawing room for coffee.

Music was being played, softly, romantically, from a tape, with speakers fixed high on the walls. An ancient castle with every modern convenience. Lorna smiled and Craig asked her why.

'I was thinking of this old castle, with all the modern aids one could wish for.'

'Yes. If our ancestors could come back, eh?'

She nodded and laughed.

'They'd be amazed, and scared.'

'Certainly they'd be scared.'

'Of the machines? I adore machines,' she confessed, and Craig lifted his brows a fraction.

'You do?'

She laughed at his half-bewildered expression.

'Machines that do all the work for you,' she elucidated.

'Ah ... dishwashers and the like?'

She nodded her head.

'Just think of all the machines one can now have in the home.'

'Woman's work is done in a trice.'

'Not quite, but there's nothing hard or back-aching about housework these days.'

Craig regarded her in silence for a moment.

'Tell me about your home in England,' he invited unexpectedly. 'You lived with an aunt and uncle, Gilbert told me.' There was little or no expression in his voice as he mentioned his friend, so it was impossible for Lorna to gain any information as to whether or not Jeff had been correct in his suspicion that Gilbert had put all the blame on her—had in fact told Craig that the engagement was at an end.

'Yes, they took me when my parents died, within six months of one another. I was only seventeen at the time. It was five years ago,' she added finally, and reflectively.

'You were young to find yourself alone.'

'Yes, but I did have my aunt and uncle.' She thought of them, taking her in—a difficult decision, she had overheard her aunt say. They had been good to her, never once revealing the fact that they did not want her. They were to be admired, and thanked, for that. But now.... They were glad to have her gone from their home, so that they could have it to themselves again. She heard Craig say, softly, enquiringly,

'What are you thinking, Lorna, to make you frown like that?'

She gave a small start and said she was not aware that she was frowning.

'I was thinking of my aunt and uncle,' she added when he assured her that she was frowning. 'They're very much in love.'

His brows lifted questioningly.

'They are?'

'I suppose that was irrelevant,' she returned in a little deprecating voice. 'What I should have said was that it's unusual to find a couple who've been married for over twenty years as madly in love as they are.'

Craig's eyes flickered.

'Some people do remain in love,' he said.

'Yes, I suppose so, but it's rare to see two people as devoted as my aunt and uncle.'

'You didn't mind leaving them, apparently?' An undercurrent of contempt in his voice? Lorna felt sure there was, and on sudden impulse she told him

that she had known that her aunt and uncle had come
to the point where they wanted to be alone again.

'How can you say that?' he asked with a frown.

She hesitated about saying what she had overheard. Craig, she felt, would be the kind of person
instantly to condemn them and this she could not
bear. So she merely passed off his question by assuring him that she knew by instinct.

'It was a sort of intuition,' she added finally.

'What about Gilbert?' he asked. 'You didn't mind
leaving him?'

She looked him in the eye.

'Craig,' she said cautiously, 'just what did Gilbert
tell you about us . . . and the separation?'

The dark eyes became veiled as Craig replied,

'As a matter of fact, Lorna, he told me the truth:
that the engagement was at an end.'

'And which one of us broke it off?'

There was a small pause and then, slowly, quietly,

'Does it matter? You both obviously realised that
marriage for you would never work, so you wisely
brought the engagement to an end.'

His answer was plainly an evasion and a frown
gathered on Lorna's forehead.

'He told you the engagement was broken by
mutual consent?'

'I don't believe he did, but that was the impression
I got at the time.'

Another evasion, but after a thoughtful pause
Lorna decided not to carry the matter any further.
She had to remember that Gilbert was Craig's friend,
and therefore she would not blacken his name. In
any case, it would not profit her anything if she did.
But she thought about Jeff's suspicions and was
puzzled, because she had accepted those suspicions

as fact, had firmly believed that Gilbert had put the entire blame upon her. She glanced at Craig, seeing his face in profile because it was half turned from her. Was he hiding something?—his expression, for instance . . .?

It was fairly late when he eventually said she ought to be leaving. His voice was low and gentle, so very different from what it had been such a short time ago! Lorna knew a surge of pleasure at the idea that he would want to walk her back to the Dower House, hoping she was not revealing this as he said,

'I'll walk with you, Lorna, and see you safely indoors.'

She looked at him with a smile, aware of the profound change that had come over her regarding her feelings for him. At one time she was sure she hated him . . . but now. . . .

It was almost a full moon that glowed in the dark hemisphere of the sky, and the grounds of the castle looked eerie and ghostly and even a little fearsome in its argent light. How easy it was to let the imagination paint pictures of bloody deeds done in time past, of the silent waiting for an attack by a marauding tribe. . . .

Craig was beside her, tall and gaunt in the moonlight, his profile angular, forbidding.

They traversed the path running alongside a massive ornamental shrubbery, and as they approached a part where shadows lurked, created by the high bushes, Craig thought it necessary to take Lorna's arm. The action was unexpected and she felt a quiver of pleasure run along her spine. Her heart was affected too, beating unevenly, in little jerks, causing a slight breathlessness within her.

'Watch your step along here,' warned Craig. 'There are one or two places where the ground lifted in the heavy frosts earlier in the year, and they haven't quite settled again yet.'

He was close to her; she could feel the movement of his body in rhythm with hers, for he had matched his pace to suit that which she was making. The contact of his hard frame did things to her; she thought of Gilbert and was filled with wonderment that he had never made her feel quite like this—no, not even in their most intimate moments.

Presently the darkness was relieved again as they came from the shadows of the shrubbery on to the path skirting one of the wide lawns. Across this great width of grassland the moon's light glowed, and the various specimen trees rose gauntly, eerily, like giants of nebulous but fearsome shape ... so silent, with not even the zephyr of a breeze to stir anything to movement. But suddenly there rang out the cry of a night-owl, piercing the quiet and sending a shudder through Lorna's body. Craig gave a short laugh and without warning his arm came about her waist, bringing her closer still, as if involuntarily wishing to comfor her.

'It's nothing to be afraid of,' he said.

'I know; I've heard the owls before. It was just the shock—I didn't expect it.' She glanced around, feeling poised in total isolation—as if she and Craig were the only inhabitants of the world.

And when again they reached a shadowed place it seemed the most natural thing for him to stop, to turn her round to face him ... to bend his dark head and kiss her.

She lay in bed, watching the sun come up, its light

filtering the space where she had not quite closed the heavy velvet drapes. Her mind was drugged with thoughts of last night. Craig had not only kissed her, but had whispered those kind of things that could mean only one thing: that he was beginning to find her attractive.

She allowed her thoughts to switch to Gilbert. It was only a few weeks since she had been madly in love with him. But he had acted so callously that he had killed her love completely. She felt nothing now, no hurt, no regrets. How right he had been when he said it was better to discover the truth now than later!

Getting out of bed, Lorna drew on a negligee and went over to the window, drawing back the curtains to let in the amber glow that came over the ridge of the mountains. The soft still peace and harmony of dawn lay over everything; the hillsides were sepia, the fields ochre-coloured but changing slowly, with the rise of the sun, to subtle colours of grey and blue and dappled pink. What peace! How far away was the hospital with its early morning bustle!—the hurry and scurry of toileting the patients, of making their beds, preparing their breakfasts, listening to their complaints and yet managing to smile.

Would she ever go back to that kind of work? By a natural process her mind became absorbed with Craig, and the way he was last night. The kisses, and especially the final one.... Colour fused her face as she thought of it, of the ardour, the mastery, the complete confidence of the man she had so recently disliked. Surely he would not act like that unless he was intending to ask her to marry him? He was certainly not the man to indulge in a light flirtation with one of his grandmother's employees. But what about this girl-friend Jeff had mentioned? She was away but returning in a few weeks' time. Lorna dismissed her as unimportant and went to the bathroom to take a shower. The scene outside was too tempting for her to linger here in the bedroom; she wanted to be in the open, enjoying the delights of nature.

She was rambling over the moors when she became aware of movement on the other side of the burn, where trees grew thickly along its bank. Craig! Her heart gave a jerk and a swift smile came to her lips. He was walking briskly, his head held high; she could imagine him taking in the air in great gulps, and exhaling slowly—exercising his lungs with the aid of the clear pure air of the heather moors. He spotted her and stopped a second before coming on towards the bridge, a smile touching the hard outline of his mouth. He was glad to see her! A warm glow fused her whole being. This was living—being in a state of mind like this ... almost in love...? Fear touched her heart with icy fingers. Supposing she were wrong? Jeff had said he did not trust Craig....

'Hello!' he called from a distance, his voice clear and firm as it came over the air. 'Couldn't you sleep?'

She laughed; she was happy, warm again, for his tone had dispelled all her fears.

'The morning was too tempting.' She was moving automatically to meet him. He held out his hands and she slipped hers into them. Lightly he kissed her.

'You look wonderful,' he said. 'What time were you up?'

'Very early—I didn't look at the time. The sun was coming over the mountains and it was all too wonderful. I had to come out.'

'You'd make a country girl,' he said, and it did seem that he was in a considering mood. 'I find it a little surprising, seeing that you've always lived in a city.'

'I've always loved the country, though.' She fell into step beside him, noticing that he slackened his pace to fit hers.

'See the hooded crows tormenting the deer?' Craig pointed, an angry note in his voice. The hateful creatures were swooping down over the heads of the lovely roe-deer, who were grazing peacefully until the hooded crows came along—a great flock appearing out of nowhere.

'I've seen them before. Why do they do that?'

'It's their way,' he answered tautly. 'They'd peck out an animal's eyes if it was ill, or too small to defend itself.'

'Don't you declare war on them?'

'Of course. Campbell, my factor, has had men searching out the nests and destroying the eggs. It's the only way to keep them down.'

'It's funny, but the other predators are so attractive, aren't they? I mean, they're so magnificent that you can't dislike them the way you do the hooded crows.'

'The falcons and eagles, you mean?' He shook his head. 'A very different matter. The eagles are most attractive birds. But they're remote for the most part, their eyries being so high up, usually on a cliff where they're safe.'

'I saw two eagles the other day, flying low over the grouse moors.' Lorna and Craig were striding out, making for the loch, shining in the sun's slanting rays. 'And I've seen buzzards and kestrels—I love the way the kestrels hover; they seem to be still, suspended in space.'

'They are suspended in space,' he returned with a laugh, and then, more seriously, 'When you see them like that it usually means death for some little creature on the ground.'

'I know, and it's sad.' A sigh escaped her and Craig turned, slanting her an unfathomable glance.

'You're—soft-hearted?'

It was a strange question, and it was spoken with what appeared to be a hint of scepticism. Lorna swallowed, aware of a hurtful little lump in her throat.

'Nurses usually are,' was all she said.

Craig made no further comment and they walked on in silence for a while, each absorbed in what was around them. To her it was still novel, but she was faintly surprised that Craig could be so interested, since it was by no means new to him.

They had disturbed the roe-deer and for a moment they stood, watching their gazelle-like leaps as they took off towards a hillock and then disappeared over the top.

'Well, at least they've got rid of the hoodies,' was Craig's rather satisfied remark. 'The birds have gone the other way—probably to find something else to torment.'

An hour passed and then, reluctantly, Lorna said she would have to be getting back to the Dower House.

'Your grandmother expects me to have breakfast with her,' she added, wondering if he knew that already.

'Do you have lunch with her?'

'No; she has both lunch and dinner on her own.'

'Yet you're her companion?'

She felt herself colour.

'I came as her nurse——'

'But she didn't need one. She told me you were now her companion——' He stopped abruptly and frowned. It was as if he regretted having brought up a matter which was bound to cause her embarrassment. 'Shall I see you this evening, Lorna?' he was saying almost immediately. 'I'll be walking after dinner as usual.'

She looked up at him, all her world rosy again.

'If—if you want to—to see me,' she began, when he interrupted her.

'You know I do, Lorna. I should miss it if you didn't walk with me.'

Words to thrill!—and to reassure her. The idea that Craig was in love with her dazed her and she tried to tell herself to be sensible, that the affair was not progressing anywhere nearly as quickly as she had been convincing herself it had. But the vague doubts did not flit through her mind for long, because Craig was pulling her to him, with a strong arm about her waist, and the kiss he gave her was possessive, his voice proprietorial when eventually he told her to meet him by the fountain in the castle grounds at nine o'clock that evening.

When she met Jeff that afternoon by the café entrance her happy expression made him ask,

'Come into a fortune or something?'

She heard the sarcasm, the petulant note and knew he was faintly jealous, and angry that she had dined with his brother-in-law's landlord.

'Shall we go in?' she said, suiting action to her words as she preceded him into the café. The table they liked was vacant and she made her way to it.

'You obviously enjoyed your evening at the castle,' was Jeff's comment once they were seated.

'Yes.' She paused a moment, feeling some further explanation was needed, but could not for one moment have told him the truth—that Craig seemed to be in love with her. 'What are we having——?' She picked up the small menu card just for effect. 'The same as usual?'

'I expect so.' Jeff caught the waitress's eye and gave the order for tea and cakes. 'I still don't trust him,' he said impatiently. 'You seem to be very naïve about this affair, Lorna.'

'In what way naïve?' She felt anger rise within her, owing to the way Jeff could, in so very few words, bring doubts to her mind.

'Well, this dramatic change—so unexpected and inexplicable. What's made him change towards you? There must be some reason.'

'I believe I told you—that he said we couldn't remain enemies when I was living so close, and in his grandmother's employ.'

'He didn't think that way at first.'

Lorna did not need reminding. She did not want to be reminded.

'I can't explain,' was all she said. 'Did you find anything out about a job for me?' She asked the question, but in her mind was the possibility that she would not be wanting a job. What, she wondered, would Gilbert have to say if his friend married her? The question had not been posed sooner simply because, these days, Gilbert never intruded into her thoughts.

'I haven't asked around,' admitted Jeff. 'You see, once I do, it'll be on everyone's tongue that you want to leave Mrs Lamond. You can't keep anything dark in a small community like this.'

'No ... it's difficult.'

'I saw Jeannie a few minutes ago,' he said, changing the subject. 'She was shopping; she looked as if she'd have liked to join us when I said you and I were having tea here.'

'Why didn't you invite her to, Jeff?'

'I suppose I wanted to be alone with you.' He stopped and gave a deep sigh. 'Forget it, Lorna. I was thinking that you and I might be more than friends, but I see now that it's not to be.'

'I'm sorry....'

'Don't fall for Craig, Lorna,' he advised, and his voice was graver than she had ever heard it before. 'He has some ulterior motive for the change that has occurred. You've admitted that there's a mystery, and you must see that Craig's changed attitude only adds to that mystery.'

There was as much logic in his words as there was anxiety in his voice, anxiety that was contagious, soon caught by Lorna, whose nerves tightened and whose common sense told her to get away from it all before she became further enmeshed. Yet how could she say goodbye to Craig at this crucial stage in their relationship?

'I can't think straight,' she told Jeff with a deep sigh. 'There's so much.' She told him about the gift of the buttons, saw his brows raise when she added the information that her employer was eager to make her a present of some of the family jewellery.

'She's either in her dotage or up to some devil-ment——' Jeff paused, frowning darkly. 'What can possibly be the reason why she wants to make a gift like that?'

'I've no idea. I intended giving her back the buttons this morning, but she was in such a black mood that I've postponed it until later.'

He looked at her thoughtfully.

'Lorna ... it does seem that she's treating you like a daughter.'

'I know, but I haven't wanted to admit it.'

'The sooner you leave the Dower House the better it will be!'

'I know that too.' She heaved another sigh as she picked up her cup and drank her tea. The cakes had not been touched, as neither she nor Jeff felt hungry. 'I'd better go,' she said presently. 'I want to return those buttons to her.'

She came out of the café with Jeff but parted from him immediately, saying she had a small amount of shopping to do.

'Okay. I'll see you tomorrow at the same time and place?'

'Of course.' She welcomed these breaks and knew she would miss them when Jeff went home in four days' time.

She had been into the stationer's and was just walking briskly in the direction of the chemist when she saw Jeannie coming towards her. Both girls produced a ready smile; Jeannie spoke before Lorna had time to do so.

'Hello! I saw Jeff and hinted that I'd like to join

you for tea, but he didn't cotton on! Is he falling in love with you?'

Lorna laughed and said no, it was absurd for Jeannie to think so.

'Are you going home now?' she asked, noticing the parcels the girl was carrying.

'In a few minutes. I've to get some groceries for Mum, but I'll put these in the car first. Can I give you a lift?'

'No, I'll walk. I've got to get some soap and talc from the chemist and then I must fly.'

Jeannie grimaced.

'Grandmother's a martinet, isn't she? I've not found out yet how you came to come up here and work for her. Perhaps you'll tell me one day, when we get to know one another better. Oh, and by the way,' she added, changing the subject abruptly, 'I've been telling Mum about you and she said I must invite you to tea on Sunday—— We have tea, I'm afraid, not dinner. Father likes his big meal at lunch time.' She looked a trifle anxious and Lorna quickly reassured her by saying,

'I'd love to come to tea, and to meet your parents, Jeannie. But what time do you have it? I usually read to your grandmother between four and half-past each afternoon.'

'Oh, not until about half-past five. You'll come then?'

'Yes—and thank your mother for asking me.'

The two girls parted, but scarcely had Lorna reached the chemists than she met Craig. One look at his face caused a shiver to run through her, for it was dark and accusing, contemptuous and scornful. His eyes seared her face as he said,

'I've been talking to Grandmother; she tells me she's made you a gift of eight gold buttons.'

Automatically Lorna nodded her head, a natural impulse in the uneasy silence that followed his words. She wanted desperately to tell him of her intention to return the gift, but knew that it could never sound convincing.

'She—told you——'

'I've just said she did!'

'I—I didn't want them, Craig,' she began, then stopped, daunted by the condemnation in his gaze.

'You accepted them nevertheless?' He paused a moment as if in indecision, and then, with another sweep of disdain that made her feel like a worm, he turned and left her standing there, tears rushing to her eyes. But very soon fury was mingling with her unhappiness; she forgot all about the toilet requisites she had meant to buy. She wanted only to confront her employer, and to tell her exactly what she thought of her. For it was plain that she had given the buttons only so that she could inform her grandson of the gift.

But why?

Everything the old lady did seemed to stem from some evil intent, and Lorna decided once and for all that she was leaving her employ.

Katie was by the side entrance to the house when Lorna arrived there.

'She's in a terrible mood,' whispered the maid conspiratorially. 'Mr Craig's been here and there was an unholy row. He stalked out looking black as thunder. I don't envy you, Miss Woodrow, having to go in there!'

Lorna looked at her intently, wondering if the girl

had heard anything Jeannie had said; she would not put it past her to listen at doors. However, there was no sign that she had overheard anything and Lorna left her, going to her room first, then to that of her employer. The old lady was seated in a straight-backed chair, an erect formidable figure, stern of feature with pale hard eyes that instantly challenged those that looked into them. Without preamble Lorna said, throwing the string of buttons on to a couch,

'There's your present, Mrs Lamond. And you can take my notice at the same time.' Lorna's mouth was set in a determined line, for although she had no idea where she would go, she fully intended leaving here. 'I'd like to leave as soon as possible....' Her voice trailed, drawn to a stop by the old woman's sudden slump in the chair, the way she fluttered a hand to her face, the sudden uncontrollable shaking of her thin gaunt body. 'Mrs Lamond! You're ill!'

'Get me on to the sofa,' the old lady gasped, fighting for breath. 'Give me one of my tablets. It's—it's another attack.'

'Yes—yes, of course.' Used as she was to moving people, Lorna found her employer to be a dead weight, and was forced to go out into the hall and call for help. It was Katie who appeared—it was bound to be, thought Lorna grimly. 'I need help with Mrs Lamond, Katie. She's had a heart attack.'

'Heart attack?' There was a scoffing note in the maid's voice, but Lorna was too concerned to notice it.

'Help me to get her on to the couch.' Lorna hurried over to it and picked up the buttons, but not before Katie had spotted them. The girl had eyes like a hawk, thought Lorna, glancing into her robust, highly-coloured face.

'There, that's better.' Katie's strength was incredible. She almost did all the weight-lifting on her own. 'She's not lost any colour, has she?' Katie looked critically at her, a half-sneer on her lips. 'Are you feeling better, madam?' she asked swiftly as she caught Mrs Lamond's expression. 'You must be careful, now,' added Katie soothingly, 'or you'll knock yourself up. Perhaps it was the excitement of seeing Mr Craig?'

The pale old eyes glinted.

'Why should I be excited at seeing my grandson, Katie?' she asked.

'Well, madam, I must be honest and admit that I heard your voices raised. Quarrelling isn't good for one, madam, and you ought to keep calm.'

'I ought to sack you, my girl. I don't know why I keep you on!'

Katie looked down, clasping her hands in front of her.

'No offence meant, madam,' she said humbly. 'I was only anxious for your welfare—just as we all are, madam.'

'Anxious, eh? Are you sure you're not anxious for me to die?'

'Oh, madam!' exclaimed the maid, horrified. 'How can you say such things! We're all devoted to you, and——'

'All right,' testily and with a feeble wave of a hand. 'Clear off. I'll ring when I want you.'

Katie went, her face turned away both from her employer and Lorna. Lorna would have given anything to see it.

CHAPTER SIX

IMMEDIATELY after the departure of the girl Mrs Lamond revived and Lorna realised at once that there had been no heart attack at all. Katie had known it, but she had not known the reason for Mrs Lamond's feigning the attack. She was sitting up on the couch when Lorna said, scorn in her voice and glance,

'It won't work, Mrs Lamond. I am not accepting any presents whatsoever from you, so you're wasting your time—and energy—in behaviour of this kind.'

The pale eyes glinted almost savagely and yet again Lorna was reminded of the barbarians who were this woman's ancestors.

'You gave me your notice! That's what brought on the attack. I can't do without you!'

'You don't need me,' argued Lorna, staring directly at her.

'I do, girl! Little you know just how much! You can't leave me now—you can't!'

'Oh, and why?' The mystery again, and Lorna felt that this might be an opportunity of gaining some knowledge regarding it.

'Because I've got used to you! I hate change—it's not good for a person of my age.' Mrs Lamond's voice changed and she was almost pleading as she added, 'Stay with me, dear. I do need you.'

Lorna hesitated, her thoughts first on the problems facing her should she throw herself out of work, but then wandering into forbidden zones.... And Craig.... He was angry, but she would explain how she came to accept the gift and he would surely understand. Would he forget the whole thing and resume their fast-growing friendship?

'You told your grandson that I'd accepted those buttons,' she said at last. 'Why did you?'

It was the old woman's turn to hesitate, and as she watched her with a keen intentness Lorna saw that she regretted telling Craig about the gift.

'I had my reasons,' she replied. And then, 'He mentioned it to you and was not pleased?' Curiously the words were framed, with a matching curiosity fixed in Mrs Lamond's eyes. 'And that's what made you give me your notice?'

'He was very angry, and it was understandable! You have no right to give the family heirlooms away to strangers!'

'You're not a stranger; neither, though, are you in a position where you can tell me what to do with my own property. I want to give you some of the jewellery——'

'Mrs Lamond,' broke in Lorna exasperatedly, 'please try to understand—and accept—my firm decision without any more argument. And let us have no more of these feigned attacks.' The old woman gave a deep sigh, which was one of resignation, much to Lorna's relief. She asked after a small silence,

'Are you thinking of leaving me, Lorna?'

'I wish I knew more about this whole business,' was Lorna's impatient rejoinder. 'I know I ought to leave you——'

'But you won't? I do need you, as I've already said.'

Lorna looked at her, not offering any assistance when she began to rise from the couch. She needed none; she had the constitution of an ox, Katie had declared more than once, and it seemed to be true.

'I'll stay for a while,' promised Lorna, thinking of Craig and knowing she would suffer more from a parting with him than she had ever done from Gilbert.

Later that evening she went into the castle grounds, hoping to meet him, but he was nowhere to be seen. With determined steps she went towards the huge front entrance to the castle, and after only the slightest pause she reached for the knocker and lifted it. The butler opened the door, nodded unsmilingly when she stated her request, then invited her in. Craig came almost immediately, his angular face grim as the dark, overcast mountains outside, his voice harshly condemning as he spoke.

'What do you want here? I've no time....' His voice trailed unexpectedly and Lorna waited, frowning in puzzlement for him to continue. 'My grandmother——' He stopped and to her amazement she saw real fear in his face. He seemed breathless as he added, 'She's...?'

'Mrs Lamond is very well.' Lorna still stared at his face, watching the features relax and the fear vanish from his eyes.

'Then why are you here?'

She paused, biting her lip. His manner was so chilling that she was regretting her decision to come here and tell him about the return of the gift. However, she did tell him, since there was nothing else she could do. His eyes lingered on her face, eyes still hard and accusing as he said, almost to himself,

'I see.... A very——' He stopped abruptly, but Lorna knew instinctively that he was going to say that it was a very clever move on her part. A clever move for what reason? So that she could find herself in his good books again? Well, it *was* the reason, but on the other hand she had no intention of humbling herself in any way.

'I just thought I'd tell you,' she added with well-assumed casualness. 'You seemed so angry that a family heirloom was being given away. I hope your mind is now at rest.' She hesitated a moment, her heart crying out for him to soften, to say something that would take away the despair which lay heavily upon her. But he merely shrugged his shoulders in the sort of gesture that could only be interpreted as a dismissal and she turned away, tears springing to her eyes. After a moment she looked back; he was striding out in the direction of the Falconer's Tower. She had meant to explain it all to him, explain how she came to accept the gift even while intending to give it back. But Craig's manner, icily scornful as it was, had been so repelling that she had no courage to say more.

The following afternoon she met Jeff and they went into the café for tea. He was morose, unhappy at the idea of having only a couple of days left of his holiday.

'You always feel like this at the end of a vacation,' Lorna said soothingly. 'It'll pass once you get into the routine of work again—at least, it always did with me.'

He looked at her and sighed.

'In a way,' he said, 'I wish I hadn't met you,

Lorna. I've come to like you such a lot that it's damned hard to say goodbye.' A small pause and then, 'Can't we write to one another?'

She shook her head.

'It wouldn't be any use, Jeff.'

'Have you seen Craig since yesterday afternoon?'

She nodded, her eyes shading.

'Yes, I saw him twice.'

'Twice?' with a lift of his brows.

She explained, her voice tonelessly automatic because she was endeavouring to keep emotion out of it. Jeff frowned as she finished, repeating even yet again that there was something very strange in the old woman's attitude towards Lorna.

'You really should think about leaving her,' he ended.

'I gave her my notice yesterday, but she begged me to stay.'

Jeff looked sharply at her.

'And you agreed to stay?'

Lorna nodded.

'It was more for my own benefit than hers. I haven't another job to go to, and I feel it's best to save some more money before leaving her.' She was frowning, troubled about her future, and at the same time desperately unhappy about the way things had gone with Craig.

'You could go back to London.'

'Not yet, Jeff——' She shook her head emphatically. 'I can't go yet—for several reasons.'

Sunday dawned bright and sunny, and Lorna wore a light cotton dress for her visit to Jeannie and her parents. She was greeted cordially and soon found herself in friendly conversation with Mr MacFarlane, his wife and daughter having gone to the kitchen to finish preparing the tea. Lorna had naturally offered to help, but had been told to stay in the sitting-room and talk to Mr MacFarlane.

Tea proved to be a most pleasant meal, with questions being put to Lorna regarding her post up at the Dower House. Mrs MacFarlane, although dignified and carrying the clear mark of the aristocrat, was so very different from her mother that it was almost impossible to believe they were even remotely related. There was no animosity in Mrs MacFarlane's voice when she mentioned her mother, but there was anxiety, reflected in her glances at Jeannie. It was plain to Lorna that the inheritance was of the utmost importance to her, not in any way for herself but for her daughter who, even now, should by rights be enjoying the luxuries of a home similar to that of her wealthy grandmother.

Jeannie insisted on walking back part of the way with Lorna, who had not stayed more than an hour after tea was over because she had not been altogether happy about Mrs Lamond earlier in the afternoon and she wanted to go to her before she retired to bed.

'What was wrong with Grandmother?' Jeannie asked when Lorna mentioned this.

'She seemed a little breathless——' Lorna stopped, not wanting to cause Jeannie anxiety. 'It's probably nothing much at all,' she added. 'I just want to make sure that she's all right, and as she goes to bed early I must get back.'

'You look after her very well,' said Jeannie.

'I don't do as much work up there as I should.'

'No? Craig says. . . .'

'Yes?'

'Nothing.'

'Craig says I get my salary for nothing?' They were walking along a narrow tree-lined lane and Lorna stopped automatically, looking into her companion's faintly flushed face.

'Don't ask me questions about my cousin,' Jeannie begged. 'As I've already told you, he's arrogant and superior and stuffy!'

'He's right, nevertheless, about me and the work I do—or, rather,' Lorna added grimly, 'the work I don't do.'

'I must admit that we were puzzled when you came —my parents and I, I mean. Craig seems to have some private theory about it, but he won't tell me anything!'

Just another aspect of the mystery, thought Lorna when eventually Jeannie had left her and she was on her own, walking up the long avenue leading to the front entrance of the Dower House. Perhaps one day it would be explained, but Lorna was becoming past caring, her one idea being to save money so that she could leave Mrs Lamond as soon as possible.

The old lady was on the couch in her boudoir, her lips faintly blue, her breathing a little strained.

'Have you had your tablets?' Lorna asked, staring down at her.

'Katie sees to them.' The old woman's voice was like a rasp and it was plain that both anger and anxiety affected her. 'Did you have a nice time at my daughter's house?'

'Very nice. They're a charming family.'

The hard eyes seemed paler and colder than ever.

'My daughter threw herself away! Disgraced the family by marrying beneath her!'

'Mr MacFarlane's one of those people whom I consider to be the salt of the earth.' Lorna's voice challenged, as did the sparkle in her eyes. She detested this woman and her arrogance, her undue assumption of superiority over those less endowed by worldly goods than she.

'You've become insolent lately,' the old woman snapped. 'Why have you changed?'

Before Lorna could reply Mrs Lamond gave a low moan and seemed to writhe on the couch. Lorna ran to the door, calling for Katie. She was there on the instant, just as Lorna expected she would be.

'I just happened to be in the hall,' she began, but Lorna interrupted, telling her to go and fetch Mrs Lamond's grandson.

'She's had an attack?' Katie ran into the boudoir and stared down at her mistress, a strange glint in her eyes. She gave a deep sigh which seemed very much like one of satisfaction rather than anxiety. 'I wanted to stay with her, but she sent me away.'

'Go and fetch Mr Lamond,' said Lorna again, picking up the telephone to ring the doctor.

Craig was there within ten minutes and the doctor five minutes later. Craig spoke privately to the doctor, after they had both seen the old lady.

'She'll be all right,' Craig was saying with an odd inflection after the doctor had left. 'But she must stay in bed for a few days.'

'I'll not stay in bed—either for you or the doctor! How does he know what I need?' Mrs Lamond wagged a forefinger in her grandson's direction. 'You're the only one who knows what I need!'

Craig's mouth went tight, but he said nothing. Lorna, troubled as she was by Mrs Lamond, had found little time to bother about Craig, but now she became aware of his intent stare and turned to meet it. His mouth moved but no words came; yet he appeared to be drawn to Lorna, who was dwelling on her employer's statement that Craig was the only one who knew what she wanted. Marriage between him and Jeannie. . . .

'Katie will look after Grandmother once she's in bed,' Craig was saying, his eyes still on Lorna. 'I want to talk to you.'

'About what?' from Mrs Lamond sharply.

'That's my business, Grandmother,' he answered softly.

'I feel it's I who should be looking after her,' said Lorna, but wondering what Craig wanted with her.

'Kindly address yourselves to me!' snapped Mrs Lamond aggressively. 'I'm not a child that you have to talk over my head! As for you, Lorna—I don't need you—or anyone else for that matter—to look after me! I'm all right—or shall be in a short while!'

Tough and no mistake, with a will of iron that appeared to be most effective in its power over the flesh.

Craig helped to get his grandmother to bed, then told Katie to remain close so that if the old lady called she would be on hand.

'I'll do that, sir,' agreed the maid at once. 'Er—is Mrs Lamond going to be all right?'

'For the present, yes.'

'Oh. . . .'

Craig glanced at her perceptively, a curl to his lips.

'Remember,' he said tautly, 'stay close.'

'Yes, sir.'

He turned to Lorna as they stood together at the top of the balustraded staircase.

'We'll walk outside,' he said. 'This place stifles me.'

'You want me to walk with you?'

Faintly he smiled.

'You seem surprised, and I don't blame you, Lorna.' He paused a moment, then gently took her arm. 'I've something important to say to you, and I'd rather say it outside.'

Her heart gave a sudden jerk, for Craig was smiling in a way that completely uplifted her spirits and sent her hopes soaring.

They were away from the grounds of the Dower House and in those of the castle when he stopped and turning to her, took her hand in his.

'I was rotten to you over that present,' he said contritely, 'but I was very angry. Then you told me it had been returned and afterwards I realised that it was the gesture of someone totally unselfish, because you knew the value of the gift.'

Lorna looked from his face to his hand, her own within it. Some strange access of uneasiness persisted despite her lightness of spirits, the result of the change in him. She was recalling Jeff's suspicions, his distrust of Craig. It was something she wanted to forget, and a moment later this was made easy because Craig was smiling tenderly down at her and saying,

'You see, Lorna dear, I soon found myself missing your company, and the walks we had.' His hand caressed hers, sending feathery ripples along her spine. 'I want you, Lorna ... for my wife.'

'Your ... wife....' Her voice faltered to silence

of disbelief. Was this miracle really happening? 'Craig,' she whispered, her mouth twisting convulsively, 'do you really mean it?'

'I really mean it, my darling.' As he spoke he turned his head from her, as if he had heard something that took away his attention. It never occurred to Lorna that he might be hiding his expression from her. She was too happy to notice anything but the fact that he was close, that he held her hand lovingly in his. . . . And in her brain rang his words, over and over again,

'I want you . . . for my wife.'

She shook her head dazedly and he laughed softly before bending his head to kiss her lips.

'It can't be true,' she faltered. 'You didn't like me at first——' She was stopped by a firm hand against her mouth.

'We'll begin from now,' he stated imperiously. 'What has gone before is of no consequence. We love each other—— Oh, yes, my dear, I know you love me; I've seen it in your eyes. We love each other, and as I've said, we shall begin from now.'

His words were music in her ears, haunting tender music through which the note of insincerity could not penetrate into senses drugged by happiness. 'We love each other. . . .'

It was a miracle that a man like the noble laird of Locharrun should have fallen in love with her and she was deliriously happy, her heart too full for her to find words, so she just snuggled close within the protection of Craig's arms and lifted her face for his kiss. The dark eyes were unfathomable; the lips were almost cruel on hers.

'Oh . . . you hurt me——'

'Sorry, darling, but I want you so badly——?' His mouth pressed to hers, forcing her lips apart. His hands moved to her hips as he brought her quivering body even closer, so that it seemed they were already one, joined in passion. 'You're so beautiful—so desirable!'

After a long time he released her, his breathing as erractic as hers. Lorna pushed her tousled hair from her face, her eyes dark and dreamy, reflecting the fire of emotion he had awakened in her. She realised that Gilbert's lovemaking was almost clinical, like his job. This was bliss even without full surrender. . . .

'Oh, Craig, I'm so happy it hurts! I love you so— and it's like a miracle that you can love me!'

He smiled faintly, and paused for a long moment before speaking. When he did speak it was to tell her quietly that the wedding would have to be a secret one, although it would take place in the private chapel of the castle, where most of his family had been married.

'But—why, Craig, must it be kept secret?' Flashing thoughts produced a vague picture of the girl mentioned by Jeff, the girl whom Craig had been interested in, and who was at present abroad.

'My grandmother.' Craig walked slowly towards a seat beneath an ancient oak tree and they both sat down, Lorna's heart a little heavy as she waited for him to continue. 'She'd never approve, and she would try to do something to prevent our marriage. Once it's done that she can't undo it. I hope you understand, my darling?' He took her hand as he spoke, and she thrilled to the touch of his lips against her throat.

'I can't just leave her and not say anything,' she began in accents of distress. 'Why won't she ap-

prove——?' Lorna stopped; she had just remembered the old lady's wish that Craig should marry
Jeannie.

'She wants me to marry my cousin.'

Lorna nodded slowly.

'Yes, I was told about her wishes.'

'However,' he said with a hint of impatience, 'her
wishes could never have materialised anyway. I love
you, Lorna, and want you now—at once! Will you
marry me as soon as I can get a licence?'

She bit her lip. There was nothing she wanted more
than to become Craig's wife, to lie in his arms, to
give of herself totally, in love and surrender. But if
her employer were to suffer an attack as a result——

'We can't, Craig,' she cried, tears starting to her
eyes. 'Supposing your grandmother were to—to die
as a result of the shock?'

His smile was almost a sneer and she turned away,
hating his expression when it was cynical like this.

'It would take a lot more than that to bring about
Grandmother's decease,' he said, something in the
timbre of his voice flashing a warning light in her subconscious that was instantly extinguished. He
sounded heartless, she thought, a little access of mis-
giving assailing her.

'She's had this attack, Craig, and it was fairly bad.'

'No such thing,' he denied. 'You might be a nurse,
Lorna, but you're not infallible. Grandmother's going to be all right; the doctor said so.'

Lorna was not convinced, even though she had
already admitted that Mrs Lamond had the constitution of an ox. Her mind was strong too, and she
knew how to use it to control her body. In fact, to
Lorna she was a rather special case, a wonderful

woman in her own particular way, a hardy Scot whose incredible strength of character had come to her in the genes of her vigorous, swashbuckling ancestors.

'I don't know what to say, Craig,' she began, aware that he was waiting for her to speak. 'I hadn't expected to have a secret wedding—I mean——'

'You'd visions of a white gown and all the fuss? I do understand, dear,' he added gently, his lips touching her pale cheek. 'But is it all that important? The actual marriage is surely what really matters, isn't it?' She nodded in agreement, and listened again to his persuasive whisperings, her body thrilling to every caress of his long brown hands as they slid from her waist to her breasts, cupping them, tightening his fingers about them. His lips too caressed as, after he had unfastened the buttons of her blouse, they found what they were seeking. And all the while he whispered to her, until at last she was won over, resigned to the secret wedding, doing what he wanted, completely controlled by a will stronger than her own.

The day of the wedding was overcast, with the mountains dark and gaunt against a sky of pewter grey flecked here and there with yellow. Strangely, Lorna found it fitted her mood. She felt cheated because she had missed all the happy weeks of planning, the flowing wedding gown, the flowers and music in the church, and even the reception, since Craig had decided that even a small wedding breakfast was unnecessary. Come to think of it, everything—just everything—had been decided by Craig.

She thought that he might have let her invite Jeannie, but that was impossible as Jeannie was away from home, spending a couple of weeks with a friend in Edinburgh, so the only people present in addition to the priest were two of Craig's most trusted servants, a couple who had been at the castle for over thirty-five years.

However, nothing could quench her excitement when at last she was at the church, looking very lovely in a lilac linen suit with a deep mauve hat, gloves and shoes. Craig was waiting, his glance appearing to be perfunctory at first, but then, his attention caught, he allowed his eyes to linger and as she gave him a smile she saw the sort of admiration that dissolved any dejection she had previously experienced.

It was all over in minutes, and Lorna, the wedding ring on her finger, was being lightly kissed by her husband.

A short while later they were at the castle, and Craig, having poured them each a glass of champagne, lifted his and said cryptically,

'Here's to the future, and the satisfactory outcome of all this.'

Lorna said frowningly,

'What do you mean, Craig—outcome?'

He looked at her, his eyes narrowed in a strange expression.

'Drink, Lorna ... to the future.' Hard the voice and even harder were his eyes. Lorna suddenly knew a great fear, a vagueness about the future that was frightening.

'I d-don't understand you,' she faltered, putting her glass down with its contents untouched. 'You're ... not the—the same. ...'

He came towards her, his manner changing with dramatic suddenness.

'Sorry, darling——' He bent and kissed her and all her world was rosy again in an instant. 'I'm a temperamental man, Lorna, and you'll have to get used to my ways.'

She stared at him in disbelief.

'I'd never have believed you were temperamental,' she said.

He looked away, putting his glass to his lips. She saw him in profile, saw the classical etching of his features—the chin, prominent and firm, the determined line of the jaw, the high cheekbone above a hollowed-out cheek, the teak-brown skin, shining, like an Arab's. A formidable picture it made, and all at once Lorna was asking herself what she had done. This man would always be her master, her supreme overlord, while her role would be that of the obedient wife, the mother of the number of children *he* decided they would have. His word would rule the entire household, his wishes were the ones that would be adhered to on every occasion. Involuntarily she shivered, and at that moment he turned back to face her.

'What is it?' he asked, curiosity in his tone but no hint of anxiety.

She said quiveringly,

'I'm—I'm suffering from—from nerves, I suppose.'

He laughed and told her to take up her glass. She obeyed, and they drank to the future.

'Put your glass down and come to me,' he commanded when they had drunk, and again she obeyed, standing there while he removed her hat and slid his fingers through her hair without regard to the expert handiwork of Katie who always washed and set Lorna's hair, though little had she known, yesterday afternoon, just what she was doing it for this time.

'You're very beautiful,' murmured Craig, bending to take possession of his wife's quivering lips. They were ruthlessly forced apart, crushed beneath his iron-hard mouth. His roving hand slid into the waistband of her skirt, pulling out her blouse; she felt the sudden warmth of his flesh as her breast was held and crushed, awakening desires whose urgency brought her body arching to his, so close that she was vitally aware of its hardness, its virility. 'I could take you to bed now,' he said in a throaty bass tone, 'but instead we've to go and face my grandmother.'

The words brought a shattering sense of reality to Lorna and she drew away, automatically tucking in her blouse.

'I'm not looking forward to that,' she shivered, reaching for her bag, in which was the comb she needed. 'She'll hate me for this.'

'And me,' he added grimly.

Lorna thought of those few hours in which she had been engaged in getting ready for her wedding. She had risen very early and put out the clothes and accessories she intended wearing, then she had taken her bath, after which she had her usual morning cup of tea, brought to her by one of Mrs Lamond's maids.

'You're up early, miss,' said the girl, glancing towards the big armchair where Lorna had placed her wedding clothes. 'Are you going somewhere, miss?'

'Yes,' returned Lorna briefly. 'Thank you for the tea.'

After drinking her tea Lorna had taken a stroll in

the gardens, then gone dutifully to take breakfast with her employer, feeling guilty and yet at the same time profoundly thankful to be leaving the Dower House and the woman whom she had come to dislike intensely. With breakfast over Lorna was normally free until eleven o'clock when—lately—she had gone in to Mrs Lamond to read to her for half an hour or so until the old lady dozed, when she would usually dismiss Lorna and tell her what time she wanted her back.

The wedding had been arranged for ten o'clock, and Lorna, alert to the danger of prying eyes belonging to Katie, had thrown a mackintosh over her suit as she left the Dower House for the castle, and her hat was carried beneath it. Lorna had thought: what a way to go to one's wedding! and she wondered if it was this that made her recall the suspicions about Craig that seemed to have become an obsession with Jeff, because he gave her another warning just before he left.

'Watch him, Lorna, for God's sake! I wouldn't trust that man as far as I could throw him!'

Mrs Lamond was sitting erect in her high-backed chair, a truly formidable figure in a black silk dress, with a black embroidered shawl thrown across her shoulders. She was staring through the window at the dark silhouette of the castle as it rose against the dull grey backcloth of the mountains, but as Lorna entered she turned her head, her pale, watery eyes widening to their full extent when she saw what she was wearing.

'You look as if you're going to a wedding—or coming from one,' she commented. 'Where...?' Slowly her voice trailed as she looked over Lorna's shoulder to the tall figure of her grandson as he entered the room and closed the door firmly behind him. 'You dressed up as well, Craig? What's going on?'

'The wedding you spoke of,' he answered cheerfully. 'Lorna and I were married about an hour ago. I hope you will wish us happy.' Coming further into the room, he took his wife's hand, holding it tightly in his. 'As you're so very fond of Lorna, having treated her as one of the family right from the first, you'll no doubt be delighted that she's become your granddaughter-in-law.'

Lorna's eyes darted to his, for there was no mistaking the ring of sneering triumph in her husband's voice, or the gleam of total satisfaction in his eyes.

'Married?' The old eyes were aghast, glowing from their sunken sockets, burning into the face of the man standing there, his manner composed, nonchalant almost. 'Married! My God!' Mrs Lamond was trembling visibly, and from her eyes in their sunken sockets there shone a fury that was venomous, matching the spasmodic clenching and unclenching of the gnarled and bony fingers. 'So you played the only ace that——'

'Lorna and I are in love,' interrupted her grandson quietly, 'so be careful what you say.'

Lorna's eyes flew to his. That he had cut the old lady short just in time was evident by the expression on his face as he returned his wife's glance. She would have given anything to know what the old woman had been about to say.

'In love . . .!' in a rasping, sceptical voice. 'She's a sly ungrateful wretch! Why, girl, the secrecy! Why? Answer me, I say!' The harsh voice quivered and broke and for a terrified moment Lorna, watching her with a professional eye, feared she would have a heart attack. But the recovery was miraculous and the voice became steady as Mrs Lamond added, 'You needn't explain the reason for secrecy; it's obvious.'

'You'd not have approved,' said Craig casually, 'and so I decided on a *fait accompli*. I don't think you would have acted any differently in those particular circumstances.'

His grandmother made a gesture of agreement. These two understood one another perfectly, Lorna decided.

'I expect that wench Katie gossiped to you?' Mrs Lamond turned her attention from her grandson to his bride. 'She told you of my wishes that Craig would marry Jeannie?'

'I learned of it,' answered Lorna, 'but not from Katie.'

The old woman shrugged her shoulders, and for a moment there was silence in the room. Lorna, still anxious about her, was noticing the drawn look on the sallow, age-lined features, the dark eyes blazing with wrath.

'Jeannie would never have agreed to marry me,' Craig was saying. 'Your ambitions could never have materialised.'

'Jeannie is of an age when she could be made to do as she was told!'

'The custom of arranged marriages died long ago,' was Craig's smooth rejoinder. 'Jeannie has a will of her own.'

And she would use it, thought Lorna, wondering what these two would have to say were they to know that Jeannie was engaged to one of Craig's estate tenants.

'I suppose,' said Mrs Lamond softly, 'you feel

you've triumphed over me?'

Craig's mouth went tight and his voice sharpened.

'I've already told you, Lorna and I are in love.'

His grandmother looked at him sceptically but said nothing. Craig became restless and soon he was saying that he and Lorna must be leaving. The old woman's lips twisted as she looked across at Lorna.

'I'm supposed to release you, I suppose?'

'My wife doesn't go out to work,' submitted Craig, gesturing towards her, then to the door. 'Come on, darling. I'll get one of Grandmother's maids to pack your belongings and have them delivered to the castle.'

Lorna paused, preferring to pack her own things. However, the implacable eyes that looked into hers seemed to deter her from arguing, and once more she was reminded that Craig's wishes were the ones that would always be adhered to.

CHAPTER SEVEN

LORNA'S clothes and other possessions arrived later
in the day. Craig had apologised to Lorna for having to be away for a few hours but assured her he
would get his business over just as quickly as he
could. There had been a telephone call just after they
had arrived at the castle after visiting Mrs Lamond,
and Lorna rather thought that it was this call which
had necessitated her husband's absence so soon after
their wedding. However, the arrival of her belongings
gave her something to do and for a couple of hours
she was unpacking and finding places for everything.
Two massive wardrobes took up some considerable
space along one wall of the bedroom, and she gave
a wry grimace on seeing her few suits and dresses in
one of them, while the other was left completely
empty. Her other articles of clothing were put away
in the drawers and when she had finished she went
into the adjoining bedroom and stood looking
around. Craig had earlier shown her the rooms, saying that he was already using this second one, but as
she had taken but a cursory glance she now looked
around her with interest. It was typically a man's
bedroom, with a massive four-poster bed, undraped,
a huge wardrobe and a sort of antique chest resem-
bling a tallboy. By the bed was an antique cabinet,
with an ormolu lamp on it and a brass carriage clock.
She saw two doors, one of which she knew led to
Craig's bathroom. The other, she discovered, opened

into a dressing-room of outsize proportions. She stared at the walk-in wardrobes and wondered if they were all filled with clothes.

She had just returned to the other bedroom when she heard a step outside the door and heard her husband's voice calling,

'Lorna, are you there?' The door knob turned at the same time and he walked in, his face dark and grim, with vivid crimson lines running upwards from his mouth.

'Is something wrong?' she wanted to know, a sinking feeling in the pit of her stomach.

'Nothing that should interest you, Lorna,' he replied with unmoved countenance. 'So you've settled in all right?'

'Yes.' A surge of uneasiness swept right through her and she felt she wanted to cry. Nerves again, she concluded, moving towards her husband and managing to produce a smile.

'Hold me, Craig,' she pleaded. 'I'm so confused— not at all what I should be on my wedding day.'

He opened his arms and soon her fears were diminishing in the comfort of his embrace.

'What's worrying you, darling?'

She lifted her head from his shoulder to look into his eyes. They seemed hard, and his mouth was a tight, compressed line in a face grim and austere.

'I love you,' she whispered, 'but—but—I don't know if—if you love m-me.' It was not at all what she had intended to say, and hearing the words she was uttering she felt shocked. What a thing to say to her husband on their wedding day!

'Silly child,' he murmured with amused tolerance.

'I shall soon be showing you whether I love you or not.'

She smiled then, but fears and doubts persisted. Why didn't he kiss her with more ardour, hold her more lovingly and possessively? Perhaps he was tired, or perhaps the business he had been conducting had been troublesome.

Dinner was a happy meal, though, with the maids really going to town with flowers and candles and bringing out all the very best porcelain and glass. Georgian silver gleamed in the candlelight, and soft music drifted down from speakers high on the walls.

Lorna had to smile as she reflected on the astonishment of the servants at the castle, only James, the butler, remaining stolidly unaffected.

'I wish you happy, sir,' he had said without so much as a smile. 'It is good, sir, that you have married.'

'What are you thinking of to make you smile so enchantingly?' Craig, immaculate in white shirt and dinner jacket, spoke to his wife from the other side of the table.

'I was thinking of the shock all your servants received when you sprang our marriage upon them.'

'Some of them would know about it at least a few hours beforehand, seeing that it was held in the chapel.'

'But the chapel's away at the other side of the grounds. I think only Mr and Mrs Wentworth would know.'

'The two who attended us? You will call them Martha and Ted.' At the hint of arrogance in his voice Lorna coloured. Meekly she said yes, she understood that she was to call the servants either by their Christian names—depending on how long they had been at the castle—or by their surnames. All the gardeners, for instance, must be addressed by their surnames, as none of them had been with Craig for more than three years.

'I don't know how I shall get used to this huge place, Craig. You'll have to be very patient with my mistakes.' Her voice, low and pleading, reflected the troubled expression in her eyes, and for a long moment she felt her husband's attention focused on her, a half frown on his brow. She heard him give a small sigh, but then he smiled at her, as if in reassurance.

'Don't worry too much,' he advised, reaching out to touch the hand that lay on the table. 'You'll soon become quite adept at being the mistress here.' The half frown reappeared; Lorna had the absurd sensation of being unwanted!

What was the matter with her? she was asking herself impatiently. It was no excuse to blame it all on nerves!

'I wish I could relax,' she said, taking one of the crusty bread rolls Craig offered her. 'I feel all tensed up and I can't explain why.'

His eyes flickered strangely.

'Tensed up? Perhaps it's because of that interview with my grandmother. It must have been rather trying for you.' He was watching her intently, his expression unfathomable.

'It was trying, as you say,' she agreed. 'I felt dreadful, letting her down like that.' She had wanted to get away from her employer, and at times there was an urgency to do so, but never had she imagined she would leave without giving in her notice. 'I don't expect she'll ever speak to me again.'

Craig said nothing to that, and for the rest of the meal he chatted to her, explaining things she might be interested in regarding her new home, with some items of its history thrown in. Many times he said something to make her smile or laugh and very soon she had forgotten all her fears, revelling in the luxury of the meal and of her surroundings. Lorna looked lovingly at Craig all the time, and was content when he gave her a smile that seemed to be a reciprocation of her own feelings.

They strolled in the castle grounds after dinner, Lorna somehow torn between excited anticipation and a sort of heaviness which, she realised, had been there all through dinner, but subconsciously.

Craig seemed to be so far away at times, coming back to her only when she said something that made him realise that he ought to be giving her more attention.

However, in a shadowed place away from the lights of the castle, he took her in his arms and for several ecstatic moments she knew the demanding fire of his ardency.

'Come, sweet, let's go in,' he murmured in a voice vibrating with desire. 'This is no time for being outdoors.'

She was undressed and standing before the mirror, combing her hair, when he came into the bedroom, clad in a dark silk dressing-gown, open at the front to reveal the fact that he wore only pyjama trousers. Aware of her own scanty attire—a diaphanous shortie nightdress which left little to the imagination —Lorna coloured delicately and lowered her head. He came in slowly, devouring every curve of her body, and took the hairbrush from her fingers.

She glanced up into his face, then gave a little inward gasp at his harsh, contemptuous expression. No, it couldn't be! She must be mistaken, imagining things! As if aware of her sudden doubts Craig smiled and drew her close, fondling her hair, her face and the lovely curve of her throat. Without speaking he lifted her up and carried her to the big wide bed which had been turned down by one of the maids. Lorna's heart was beating overrate as his hands roved, caressing every curve of her quivering body. A great surge of desperate longing swept over her as he crushed her breasts, pressing the nipples between his hard fingers.

'God, but you're desirable, Lorna!' he breathed, his mouth like fire on her lips, his hands roving to more intimate places. 'I've never wanted a woman as I want you at this moment!'

Want.... Why hadn't he said he loved her? She thought for a moment that she would insist that he said it, then squirmed at the idea. He did *not* love her. In this—what should have been the first of many delirious interludes in their married life—she knew without any doubts at all that he did not love her.

She twisted beneath him, wanting to speak, but words failed her, crushed by disillusionment. Craig meant to make love to her, had reached a point of no return, so any protest on her part, any attempt at a showdown, would be ignored.

Why had he married her? She was asking this even as, having discarded the only two garments he wore, he lay down beside her. She would ask him tomorrow....

Tomorrow.... Tears stung her eyes, but he failed to notice, his face being buried between the warm curves of her breasts. She could not respond to his lovemaking at first and he seemed to become faintly angry. She was afraid of him, and when he ordered her to caress him she had to obey. And then his body was on hers, his dominance arrogantly displayed as he took her without one word of endearment leaving his lips.

Lorna lay awake for hours after Craig was breathing smoothly, obviously enjoying an untroubled sleep. What had she done? More important, what moves must she made to undo it? Why had Craig married her? Why had she allowed him to rush her into it? Was it eagerness to leave her employer that had influenced her? So many questions scattered about in her brain, not one of which she could answer.

She turned, tossing about, feeling she would give anything to be free again, on her own, in a bed where there would be no contacts that she did not want.

At last she slept, but fitfully, and she was awake again as the sun came up. She turned her head, saw the dark contented face of her husband and fury rose within her.

An hour later, after she had bathed and dressed, she was by the dressing-table, saying over her shoulder,

'Perhaps, Craig, you'll tell me why you married me?' She watched him in the mirror, saw the slow sneer that flitted across his handsome face, noticed the casual manner in which he raised himself up on an elbow, the better to see her.

'So you know I don't love you?' His steely gaze never changed as his eyes met hers through the mirror. 'It was inevitable, seeing that you're such a clever woman. What puzzles me about you is why you took up such a noble profession as nursing. I should have thought you'd have seen the advantage of an altogether different career.'

She swung around, a silver-backed hairbrush in her hand which she had the greatest difficulty in not flinging at him. She seemed not to be feeling any pain even though her heart was near breaking. The sneering arrogance of him, the implication of his hateful words, the total lack of emotion when his first sentence was spoken ... all these robbed her of feeling; it was like being numbed, but aware that pain, excruciating and prolonged, would be the aftermath of this lack of feeling within her.

'You can keep your insults, Craig! All that interests me at the moment is your reason for marrying me.'

'I married you,' he replied slowly, 'in order to thwart my grandmother. You're well aware now that she was changing her will in your favour. She had already seen her lawyer and asked him to draw up the new will. For myself, I'm indifferent, although I'd have done anything in my power to prevent you succeeding in your avaricious intention,' he added unpleasantly. 'However, the change of will would have affected my cousin and I wasn't having that! Jeannie's mother lost everything, but that's no reason why the girl who would have been her heir should also lose. Grandmother's will at present benefits both Jeannie and me; had she changed it then we'd both have lost everything, to you. As it is now, Grandmother will never leave her fortune to you, simply because she knows it would eventually come to me —when she dies, that is. She'll now make Jeannie her sole beneficiary, and that's as it should be, since her mother ought to have inherited Grandmother's wealth.'

He looked down into Lorna's pale face and for a fleeting instant there seemed to be regret written there. But then the mask was drawn again and there was a merciless quality in his voice as he added, 'You're a no-good, Lorna, so you've received only what you deserve. You threw Gilbert over when Grandmother offered you a life of luxury; you've lived like a lady, and although you gave back the present she made you, it was only another move in your little game. You believed I was falling in love with you and as you had no idea that Grandmother's fortune might eventually be yours, you decided to marry me. Don't put on that stricken expression, Lorna,' he sneered, 'it won't work. I'd never be deceived in a woman like you.' He paused, but she could find nothing to say as she tried to go over all he had told her. 'My only regret is that I've had to sacrifice myself in marrying you. But we can do something about that, later, when Grandmother dies.'

He half-turned from her and she stood looking at his arrogant profile, still unable to speak as she continued to ponder all he had said. He had used her for his own ends, thwarting his grandmother who had intended using her for *her* own ends. Lorna suddenly hated both of them ... and she hated Gilbert even more. She had been made a pawn, something to be pushed around to suit the whims and wishes of others. She swallowed, so angry that the idea of trying to defend herself never presented itself to her. What good would it do anyway? Craig had no love for her, so why bother to clear herself? He had his own ideas concerning her character, based originally on Gilbert's lies, and she had the sound conviction that those ideas were firmly set and that nothing she could do or say would clear her in her husband's eyes. How very right Jeff had been!—both about the old lady and her grandson.

'Have you nothing to say?' Craig's voice drifted through her unhappy thoughts and she looked at him, noticing even now the attraction of his features, the way his hair, tousled from contact with the pillow, fell on to his forehead. Despite her hatred for what he had done to her she could not remain immune to his magnetism; it drew her, so that she was vitally aware of the deep love she had for him, a love surpassing by far anything she had felt for Gilbert.

'I've nothing to say to you at present,' she managed at length, amazed at the calmness of her voice. It would probably mislead him, she thought mechanically, but as his opinion of her could not become any lower she did not let the circumstance trouble her. In fact, she was still in a sort of wraith-like void where feelings were almost totally lacking in strength— yes, she knew a hatred for those who had used her, but the numbness remained for the most part. It was, she decided, something like delayed shock after an accident or some other calamity. Sooner or later she would begin to *feel*, and to suffer. 'I shall have to think what I must do,' she added finally, seeing the sudden lift to his straight dark brows.

'You're not thinking of leaving me.' A statement and yet a question too. He seemed anxious, as if he did not want her to leave him. And all at once she realised that this was understandable, since it would reveal so much to his grandmother—in fact, it would reveal everything regarding his schemes to thwart her in her plans to change her will.

'I've already said I must think what to do. I might leave you——'

'You can't! You shan't!'

'So you're troubled, are you?' It was Lorna's turn to produce a sneer. 'Don't you think, Craig, that it would have been more prudent for you to have kept up the deception a while longer? Or perhaps it was a terrible strain for you to act as if you loved me when in reality you—you h-hated m-me....' Her voice failed her, caught by the terrible lump that was rising in her throat. 'You said you knew I loved you, but that too was a ruse, wasn't it?' How little he knew that he had hit on the truth even though he was acting a part. 'Well,' she said presently, determined to strike back at him, 'you know that I don't love you ... and never could!'

He shrugged, his glance of indifference a knife twisting in her heart.

'We've both benefited by the marriage,' he said, unmoved by the brightness suddenly appearing in her lovely eyes. 'I shall not be found too mean, when the time comes for us to say goodbye.'

She looked at him mistily, her instant reaction to be a swift denial that she wanted anything from him. But she was so hurt that she could only think of retaliation and she flung at him the firm assertion that she would fight for her rights.

'I shall demand a share in your capital and your income!' she added in tones sharp with anger. 'The law looks after the divorced wife these days, remember. It might cost you dear for this!—especially if Mrs Lamond leaves everything to Jeannie, as you be-

lieve she will!' Without giving him time to reply she
flounced past him to the door, where she turned to
throw her parting shot. 'I might just go to your
grandmother and tell her everything——'

'By God, you won't!' With a cat-like leap he was
beside her, gripping her wrist so painfully that she
cried out. 'Do that, wife, and I'll make you smart for
a month!' He would, too, she decided, her heart
pounding against her ribs. 'Take good care, Lorna,'
he warned in a much quieter voice, but one that was
still as menacing. 'You scarcely know me—and what
you don't know about me is something damned unpleasant—do I make myself clear?'

'Perfectly clear,' she answered, staring disbelievingly at the crimson blotch left on her wrist by the
pressure of his thumb. It would bruise, she thought
dazedly, wondering how she could have fallen in love
with a man who was as cruel as the barbarians from
whose ancestral line he had sprung.

Craig avoided her for the rest of the day, being away
at lunch time when she went to the dining-room for
her midday meal. Not that she felt like it, but she was
being careful—for the present until she had sorted
herself out—not to do anything that would appear
strange in the eyes of the servants. All the morning
she had been going over everything Craig had said,
unravelling more of the tangled skeins of the mystery
which she had never believed she would solve, but
which had been solved for her by her husband this
morning. She had strolled into the grounds, far from
the castle itself, and had found a quiet place beside a
little burn and sat down on a convenient boulder and
begun at the beginning when Gilbert had seemed to

be hiding something from her.

He had obviously told his friend that his grandmother had made Lorna a generous offer of a 'cushy' job and Lorna, lured by the money and the leisurely life, had not hesitated to throw him over. Craig had consequently despised her even before she arrived in Scotland, so she now understood his manner with her on that first day when he had driven her from the railway station to his grandmother's home. From then on he had not hesitated to throw out scornful barbs at her whenever they met. He had obviously heard from his grandmother the threat to make Lorna her beneficiary if he and Jeannie remained adamant regarding her wishes. The wily old bird had not had any qualms about using Lorna, but Lorna was under no illusions that the old woman would carry out her threat and make Lorna her heiress. In fact, she had already gone a long way to doing just that: she had seen her lawyer. The gifts—well, Lorna could see why she wanted to give her some of the family jewels. It was to prove to Craig that she meant what she said regarding her intentions towards Lorna. Craig had remained firmly against obeying the old woman and, made of the particular stock that she was, it had riled her to the point where she had resigned herself to cutting him off, but she had also intended cutting Jeannie of as well—a dastardly act, seeing that Jeannie knew of her grandmother's wish that she and Craig would marry; she knew nothing of the threat to cut them out of her will.

Craig had condemned Lorna for coming here, and —so he supposed—ingratiating herself with the old lady for the sole purpose of profit.

What Craig did not know was that she, Lorna,

would never have accepted the legacy and therefore both he and his cousin would have come into what was rightly theirs.

Bitterness became Lorna's one consuming emotion, leaving room for no others. She knew she would always love Craig but had no intention of allowing it to ruin her whole life. Her profession as a nurse had inured her to some extent against adversity, since she had come up against the troubles and distress of others all the time. She would suffer over this, but she was determined to recover from it. Life would go on; she would be free eventually, and although at this moment she felt certain she would never ever look at a man again, she did realise that time was the most effective healer.

Craig put in an appearance just before dinner-time; Lorna was in the bedroom, having just taken a shower and got dressed in a long skirt and evening blouse of coral lace.

She turned as he entered from the other bedroom, swivelling round on the dressing-stool.

'Did you have a good day?' she asked with the deliberate intention of being politely conversational.

'Fair. I'd some business with my factor.'

'And I expect you saw your grandmother?'

His eyes glinted for a brief space.

'What makes you suppose that? Have you been over to the Dower House today?'

She shook her head.

'No, but I rather thought she would have sent for you.'

'I saw her yesterday, after our visit.'

So that was where he had gone, and that was why he appeared to be angry when he returned. They had

had a quarrel, obviously.

'Did you tell her that you'd got married in haste so that she wouldn't change her will?'

'I did not! What exactly are you getting at?' He was standing in the doorway, a formidable figure in riding jacket and a black rollneck sweater. 'I'd told her we married because we were in love.'

'She didn't believe you and you know it. However, that isn't important, is it? She had a heart attack and it was then that you realised you would have to marry me quickly, as she could have changed her will and then died, leaving me her legatee. So you assumed an attitude of contrition, apologising for being so hateful to me over that gift when you'd refused to believe that I wasn't a mercenary, grasping woman who intended taking all she could get her hands on. Yes, Craig, you realised you'd have to change towards me, and I like a fool took it all in.' She stopped, aware that she had spoken as if she cared for him, which was the last impression she wanted to give. 'At least,' she amended swiftly, 'you were under the impression that I took it all in, but of course, as I was scheming too, I had to make it appear that I was taking it all in.' Again, she stopped, this time because he was looking at her so strangely.

'Aren't you getting rather muddled?' he said with an odd inflection in his voice. 'Did you take it in or didn't you?'

'I pretended I did.' She turned away, profoundly conscious of his close scrutiny, his eyes registering a question, and she had no intention of giving away the hurt she was feeling, or the lie she was telling as a result of it.

'I see. . . .' He spoke softly, and without warning he

took her chin in his hand and made her face him.
Lorna compressed her lips, knowing that it was often
the mouth—and not the eyes—that could reflect a
person's feelings. It was another thing that she had
learned in her occupation as a nurse. People in pain,
whether it be physical or mental, often moved their
lips convulsively. Craig's compelling gaze held hers
for a long moment and then, without warning, he
bent his head and kissed her hard on the mouth. She
kept hers tight, and the action angered him to the extent that he swung her into his arms, imprisoning her
so that there was no escape, then he pressed his
mouth sensually to hers, arrogantly compelling her to
part her lips by the sheer pain he inflicted in the process. His lips were hot, firing her with a desire she
strove vainly and desperately to fight. He laughed
softly and with triumph as she pressed to him, curving her yielding body to the pressure of his hand on
her back.

'It's almost dinner-time,' he sighed, glancing at his
watch. 'Pity. However, in a few hours——'

'Do you suppose I want you making love to me
now!' she blazed, breaking from him and running to
the other side of the room. 'You can forget it!' she
added. 'I'm not a convenience for you! I believe
you've someone else who might oblige!'

'Someone——!' Craig stared at her, his eyes
ablaze. 'What do you know about someone else?'

'The woman whose father has the estate adjoining
yours. You'd have married her if you hadn't of neces-
sity had to marry me. I wonder what she's going to
say when she returns from her trip abroad?'

'So the gossips have had their tongues wagging,
and you've listened. Was it Katie, or that young man

you became friendly with?'

'It doesn't matter. What I was saying was that I'm not willing to sleep with you any more. I don't want you—get that!'

'You'll sleep with me all right,' he told her in a very soft voice. 'You married me for what you could get. By your own admission you intend to get all the law can give—later, when we're divorced.' He spoke in low, threatening tones, approaching her as he did so. 'And so, my girl, you'll give me something in return.' He was near her, suffocatingly so, and as she tried to dodge past him he caught her by the waist, swinging her close, arching her body till she thought her back would break. 'There'll be no shirking, Lorna, and the sooner you accept that the better it will be for you!' His mouth was close; she twisted about, fighting him with every bit of strength she had. But it was futile; he possessed her mouth with brutal arrogance, not drawing away until she was fighting for breath. 'A lesson for you,' he told her unpleasantly. 'I advise you to learn it, for your own good. I'm your master and it's my will that you'll regard.'

'I won't sleep with you!' she cried when presently she was free. 'I shall not!'

'We'll see.' Again he glanced at his watch. 'I'll see you at the dinner-table,' he said, and disappeared into his room.

Lorna stood irresolute, her whole body shaking. Undoubtedly Craig could awaken desires in her so strong that she could never resist him. And yet she felt sullied even by the vision of his mastering her, compelling her to respond to his lovemaking. How well he read her! She coloured with humiliation, putting cool hands to her cheeks and realising after a

moment that there were tears dropping on to them.
What was she to do? Run away? But where would
she go at this time of the evening? There were neither
trains nor buses, and she had no other form of trans-
port. She felt trapped, desperate for a means of
escape. But as the moments passed she was accepting
that there was none—at least, not tonight. In the
morning, though, she would leave, go back to her
aunt and uncle for the time being. She had written
them a letter telling of her marriage but had not yet
posted it; she decided not to tell them she was married. There was no need for them to know because
as soon as she could she would leave them again—
find herself a flat or room somewhere. The divorce,
when it came, would go through quietly and they
need never know she had ever been married.

'I wouldn't use his name anyway,' she was saying,
aloud, when Craig re-entered the room.

'What was that?' he demanded, giving her a dark-
ling stare.

'Nothing that would interest you!' she snapped.

'You were saying something about not using my
name. Why was that?'

He was curious to know the idea behind the
words. She had no intention of telling him what was
in her mind.

'I merely said that, once we've parted, I shan't use
your name.'

He looked searchingly at her.

'I don't believe that was what you meant, Lorna,'
he said.

'Do I care what you believe or don't believe?' She
looked at the clock on the bedside cabinet. 'It's time
we were going down.'

'Why have you been crying?' he asked, ignoring her words.

'I haven't been crying,' she was swift to deny. 'There's something wrong with my eyes; they've been watering.'

His keen scrutiny remained on her for a long moment before he spoke.

'You're a puzzle to me, Lorna,' he said with a touch of asperity. 'Are you all bad, I wonder?'

'As far as you're concerned, yes. I'm all bad!'

'Which is in itself a denial.'

'Interpret it the way you wish. I couldn't care either way.'

'I wonder....' he murmured strangely. 'I wonder if you're...?'

'If I'm in love with you?' She laughed harshly and saw him frown. 'Women of my brand don't do anything so stupid as falling in love, Craig!'

Silence, long and profound. Craig seemed undecided, opening his mouth to speak, then closing it again. 'You're right about our going down to dinner,' was all he said, and he led the way to the door.

The meal was delicious, the wine heady. Candles and flowers abounded again, the servants providing the romantic setting which they in their ignorance felt was necessary. Lorna, sitting opposite her husband, watched him intently, aware of some change in him, but a change so slight that it was impossible to say what it was. He was quiet, thoughtful, and his eating was often mechanical. Had his grandmother been saying something disturbing to him? Or was it something on the estate——? Lorna cut short her musings, instinctively knowing that she was on the wrong thought wave. It was something very personal to himself that was affecting her husband, and to her amazement she found herself wishing he would confide in her, let her help him sort out whatever it was that troubled him. He glanced at her and she wanted so much to smile, but instead she looked down at her plate, and began to eat her fish. The music was playing, the scent of roses drifted over the table, the candlelight was golden. Suddenly she was full up inside, achingly aware of the void where companionship ought to have been, of the absence of happy conversation between them ... and of the endearments they ought to have been passing to each other had their marriage been one born of love. Tears stung her lids, but she fought them back. Craig looked at her and said,

'You're not thinking of leaving me, are you, Lorna?'

She gave a perceptible start and saw his look become perceptive.

'You don't expect me to stay, do you?' she asked.

He frowned as he said,

'You can't leave me yet, not while Grandmother lives.'

'Mrs Lamond could live to be a hundred,' she returned, but had her doubts, now that the old lady had had that last attack.

'I don't believe she'll last the year out,' he said, and something in his tone made her say,

'You were with the doctor after the attack. What did he tell you? You said she was going to be all right, but. ...'

He nodded.

'You've guessed. The doctor didn't say she was

going to be all right. He said in fact that she could go any time.'

'Any time. . . . So I was right when I said that you'd been forced to move quickly, to marry me without delay.'

'Of course; I've not attempted to deny it.'

'So the will hasn't been altered? You and Jeannie are still her heirs?'

'At the moment, but I expect she'll lose no time in cutting me out. Jeannie will get everything.'

Lorna said nothing. Craig was gloating, probably, and feeling satisfied with himself for disclosing to her that she was to have been the heiress to a vast fortune. Well, let him bask in his satisfaction! The fact was that she had lost nothing, simply because she would never have accepted a penny of the money, but Craig would never know this, for she would never tell him, knowing that he would merely sneer and tell her she was lying.

CHAPTER EIGHT

THE next morning Lorna rose very early, bathed and dressed, then went down to peruse the telephone directory. She would phone for a taxi later, when Craig had gone out to see his factor. She hoped he would stay away long enough for her to make her escape unhindered, and she was optimistic about this because the estate was so vast, covering several thousands of acres of grouse moors alone, that Craig could be gone for hours.

At breakfast she and Craig said little to one another, but several times she caught him looking at her, an odd expression on his face. Last night she had gone to him willingly, and she supposed he was puzzled as to why she had not put up a fight after what she had said earlier about not sleeping with him. He said, after a while,

'What are you going to do with yourself today, Lorna?'

Her lashes fluttered down.

'I expect I shall read, or perhaps take a long walk. You——? Shall you be away all morning?'

'Until about eleven, that's all.'

Eleven. . . . So if she had the taxi come at ten then she would be away long before he returned.

As soon as he left she phoned the taxi firm and then the railway station, being fairly certain there was a train to London somewhere around midday.

'Eleven fifty-five,' she heard the clerk saying, and

after thanking her Lorna went upstairs to pack. The maid had already done the room, so there was no danger of Lorna's being interrupted. All went well, and her suitcases were packed and standing by the door when she remembered a bracelet that must have been left at the Dower House. It was gold, the only really valuable piece of jewellery she possessed. It had been given to her by an old lady, a friend of her aunt who had since died. Lorna stood before the dressing-table, a frown of indecision on her forehead. Should she go and collect it, or write to Mrs Lamond asking for it to be posted on to her? Lorna could understand how it came to be missed by the maid who did her packing, for she, Lorna, had put it, in its box, at the back of a high shelf in the wardrobe.

'Oh dear, what shall I do?' She had about twenty minutes before the arrival of the taxi ... but it might come early. However, she decided to go and collect the bracelet, calculating that if she ran all the way there and back she would manage it quite comfortably. But supposing she was interrupted and kept talking by Katie?—or even Mrs Lamond? There was even the possibility that her former employer would keep her talking—giving her the telling off which she thought she deserved—but Lorna rather thought the woman would not even see her.

She arrived at the front entrance breathless, and was relieved to see the housekeeper open the door.

She explained what had happened; the housekeeper went off at once to collect the bracelet, but before she returned Katie appeared and said, in a very loud and excited voice,

'Oh, what a fortunate thing for you to be here, Miss—I mean Mrs—— It's the old lady! She's just collapsed and I was going to get some help and then run over to the castle to tell Mr Craig—— But you'll take a look at her, won't you, Mrs Lamond?' Katie coloured slightly as she spoke Lorna's married name, but Lorna was not taking any notice of the girl, her brain counting the minutes in a sort of feverish indecision. 'And I'll fetch Mr Craig.'

'I can't, Katie....'

Can't.... She *could* see the old lady. All Lorna's professional obligations came to the forefront of her mind and she stepped past the girl, asking as she did if Mrs Lamond was in her boudoir.

'Yes, and she's very ill!'

Lorna spared her a swift look; the girl was excited ... hopeful. Suddenly it was pity Lorna was feeling for the woman whose intention it had been to use her, for she would end her long life without anyone regretting her passing. Not one of her servants cared if she died this minute. Katie, and most likely others, wanted her to die, expectantly believing they would be left a legacy.

As Katie said, Mrs Lamond was very ill. She gasped for breath and Lorna heard it even before she got anywhere near the room. Her lips were dark purple, her eyes glazed and staring.

But she recognised Lorna as soon as she approached the big sofa on which she lay, her head against the cushions.

'You! Who brought you here?' she demanded, her voice harsh despite its weak tone.

'I just happened to come for something that had been left behind,' Lorna explained gently. 'Mrs Lamond, I'm phoning for the doctor. Katie's gone to fetch your grandson.' She phoned at once, and as she replaced the receiver Mrs Lamond said,

'Your husband, eh?' The old lady actually tried to ease herself up, but Lorna firmly kept her where she was. She was all concern, for the woman's case was grave, very grave. The taxi coming.... And Katie going to fetch Craig.... It seemed very much as if there was to be a showdown with her husband, since it was now impossible that she could leave without his knowing. Oh, well, she thought resignedly, it didn't matter all that much. She intended leaving anyway, and she could not conceive how he could prevent her from doing so.

Mrs Lamond was speaking, her accents so weak that Lorna had difficulty in catching what she said.

'You—did m-me a dastardly—trick—after all I'd d-done for you——' The voice cracked to silence and Lorna, her hand on Mrs Lamond's wrist, watched anxiously, fearing the end was so close that neither the doctor nor Craig would arrive in time.

'Just try to relax,' she advised when she saw that Mrs Lamond was again trying to speak. 'Craig will be here directly——'

'I don't want Craig—I hate him for going against my wishes. And—and you—betrayer that—y-you are——' A gasp that was almost a deep-rooted sob escaped her, but even yet again she rallied and was able to continue, 'You let him—him persuade you to m-marry him, and I suppose you believed he loved you?' A laugh escaped through the tight, papery lips and when she spoke again her articulation seemed almost normal. 'Well, you're going to get your deserts, my girl! He doesn't love you; he married you because he knew I intended to make you my heiress! He's always disliked you—and he's had reason. He was jealous of the way I treated you. I brought you here to use you——' She broke off, gasping for breath. Lorna said quietly, smoothing the wispy hair from her damp forehead,

'Don't talk any more, Mrs Lamond. I know everything, you see, because Craig told me himself that he married me to spite you.' She paused a moment, looking down at her, pity mixing incongruously with intense dislike. 'You had no right to decide to give away your fortune to a stranger. You inherited it in the first place and it was for your own family, not a total stranger like me.'

'Conscientious, eh?' A weak laugh broke. 'I wonder if you're really sincere. I expect Craig believes you married him for money and position, but he could be wrong. But no matter,' she added impatiently. 'It's not going to worry me because I'm at the end. However, I've got the best of the three of you. I've had my lawyer here early this morning—eight o'clock, which made that wench Katie curious, I'll bet! I've left my money to charity!'

'Charity!' gasped Lorna disbelievingly. 'But you can't do a thing like that! What about Jeannie?' She was almost in tears, immeasurably distressed at the idea of Jeannie being cut out of the will completely. 'You must alter it again——'

'What about Jeannie, you say?' the old woman spat out. 'She's another who's let me down! Gone the way of her wretched mother and got herself engaged to a mere labourer!'

Lorna stared in sheer dismay.

'How do you know about the engagement?' she asked.

'*You* know about it?' queried Mrs Lamond curiously, and Lorna nodded.

'Yes—but how do you come to know?'

'Katie; who else would delve into the doings of my

granddaughter and come out with the secrets? She
had the nerve to tell me, but though I was grateful to
her I cut her out of my will! She's always expected a
nice little legacy, but....' Her voice trailed and she
gave a weak little gasp. The next moment Lorna
knew that she was going into a coma. Craig arrived
just as she lost consciousness and the doctor was only
seconds behind him.

'She'll not come out of the coma,' he stated, shaking his head. 'She could last for a few hours or even
days, but she'll never regain consciousness.'

Immediately he had gone Craig helped Lorna to
get his grandmother to bed. The housekeeper also
lent a hand, looking stolid and serious, and if she
felt any emotion she hid it effectively beneath the
taut mask.

'How do you come to be here?' Craig wanted to
know when, having left Katie sitting by her mistress's
bed, they were both in the sitting-room. 'You came
in order to talk to my grandmother?'

So he hadn't seen the taxi-driver, obviously. Katie
must have found him before she reached the castle.

'I came for a bracelet which got left when my packing was done.'

'I see. Very fortunate that you did happen to be
here.'

'I couldn't do anything,' Lorna said indifferently.
'She was conscious, and talkative at times, but I saw
at once that her condition was serious. I merely
phoned for the doctor while Katie went to find you.
There was nothing else I could do for your grandmother.'

'She was talkative, you say?'

Lorna nodded her head.

'Sometimes her voice was not very clear,' she returned evasively, 'and I had difficulty in catching her words.'

His dark eyes fixed hers steadily, suspicion in their narrowed depths.

'Are you hiding something, Lorna?'

'She talked mainly about you, but she told me only what I already knew—that you'd married me to spite her, and to make sure I didn't benefit from her will.'

'Did she mention anything about changing her will?'

Lorna hesitated, for some indefinable reason loath to tell Craig that the money that had caused all the trouble was going to charity. He would know soon enough, of course, but Lorna had no wish to be the one to tell him. For one thing, she could not regard herself as one of the family, even though she was married to Craig. Her marriage seemed a vague and temporary thing that should never have happened; it would end soon and they would both be as free as they were before. Despite her bitter assertion that she meant to make him pay, she had no intention of taking one penny from him. She had managed to live very comfortably before and she would do so again, depending on no one but herself and her ability to provide for all her needs.

He was regarding her searchingly and she said, adopting a casual manner,

'She did say something about a will, but as I said, her speech was very bad at times.'

It seemed that he would pursue the subject, but to Lorna's relief he decided not to do so.

'There's nothing we can do here,' he said, 'so we might as well go home.'

Home.... She swallowed hard, her throat constricted. Home.... The castle was not her home and he knew it. She said huskily,

'I'm leaving you, Craig. I'd have been gone already if this hadn't happened. I'd phoned for a taxi, which was to arrive at ten o'clock. I came here for the brace-let——' She stopped, spreading her hands. 'The taxi will have gone, and in any case I've missed the train, but I'm leaving just the same. I can stay in an hotel for tonight and travel to London tomorrow.'

She turned away to hide her expression, but he brought her round to face him, gripping her wrist so tightly that she winced.

'You'd planned to leave this morning?' he said harshly.

'Yes, Craig, I had.'

He released her and she moved away to the other side of the room and stood with her face half turned to the window. Rising against the hills the outline of the ancient castle appeared dark and forbidding ... like its owner, thought Lorna, glancing at him.

'So you're a shirker as well as the rest,' he said contemptuously. 'You married me for money and now you're not willing to give anything in re-turn——' He cut off suddenly, staring at her with a narrowed gaze. 'There's something about you that I can't fathom, no matter how I try.'

'Then don't try,' she recommended, her voice cool because she was very successfully managing to hold her emotions in check. But the tears were close and the weight in her heart was almost a physical sen-sation, a sickening, despairing ache which she felt would never lighten. 'It's scarcely important that you understand me, is it, seeing that our marriage is al-ready finished.'

Craig swallowed hard, as if clearing something uncomfortable from his throat.

'You can't leave yet,' he said, and now his voice was quiet, persuasive almost. 'Wait until Grandmother goes——'

'Why? What difference will it make?' She stared at him curiously. 'You don't really want me, so why the reluctance to let me go?'

'Don't want you?' His eyes roved her body, dark eyes and sensuous in their expression. 'I've said you're the most beautiful woman I've ever met. Of course I want you ... and you want me, physically.'

She coloured hotly and turned from him. He came across the room with three or four swift strides and caught her in his arms before she had time even to grasp what he was about. Her head was tilted back; she stared fascinated into his eyes as his head came down, slowly, his lips seeming to thicken as they parted, meeting hers in a long and possessively brutal kiss. She struggled even while ecstasy swept through her as his hand sought and crushed one firm and tender breast. His other hand was on her back, sliding down beneath the waistband of her skirt.

'Leave me,' she implored, 'let me alone.'

'You want me—say it,' he commanded imperiously, but she shook her head and tried to break loose from the hawser-like hold. He laughed, bent his head again and took her lips, parting them by force, exploring in gentle, sensuous movements. Her body arched to meet the powerful hardness of him, desire awakened by the compelling, confident force of the willpower he was exerting over her. 'Say it,' he ordered again, his mouth against her ear. 'I shall make you, Lorna ... and it won't be with a great amount of effort.' He held her from him, his lips curving in a satirical smile. 'Why don't we both have a bit of enjoyment from this marriage, before we break it up?

After all, if we part now you're going to look as great a fool as I shall.'

She managed to free herself as his hold on her arms slackened, and she stepped back, away from him, her face pale but desire for him still searing through her entire body and mind.

'So that's all that's troubling you,' she said huskily, 'the humiliation, the gossip by your servants, the questions your friends will be sure to ask. Well, Craig, you should have thought of that before you married me, shouldn't you?' He made no answer, merely studying her closely, the most odd expression on his face. 'As for me—well, as I haven't told anyone of the marriage I'm not going to look a fool at all. Even my aunt and uncle don't know of it.'

His eyes flickered; she had the impression that he had not heard what she had said, that he was absorbed by his keen examination of her features. She knew he had forgotten that he said he would make her admit she wanted him as he said,

'You don't talk like a woman whose main object in life is to get her hands on someone else's money. In fact, Lorna, I do believe you care for me——'

'Care!' She threw him a jeering, contemptuous glance. 'What an opinion you have of yourself, Craig! Pompous ass, to think for one moment that I would fall in love with a man like you!' She laughed in his face, desperately hoping she had disillusioned him. It would be the supreme humiliation of it all if he were to guess she was madly in love with him. 'Go and have another think,' she added derisively. 'Your guess was right the first time! I married you for what I could get out of it, and as I've already said, I'll squeeze every penny out of you when the divorce goes through! A wife can get half of everything un-

der the new laws,' she added, her one object to derive
satisfaction from scaring him. 'You'll be forced to
give me half—and to make me a generous allowance
for the rest of my life.' She was quivering from the
vehemence of her words but managed to continue,
assuring him that he would regret having used her for
his own ends. Carried away as she was in her en-
deavour to hit him right between the eyes, it never
occurred to her that the content of her words was a
contradiction in itself, a revelation which she had
missed but which Craig certainly had not. He stared
for a space and then said, his eyes portraying a mixture of perception and puzzlement, each at variance
with the other,

'You're ... hurt....' He shook his head, an automatic gesture. He seemed a trifle dazed, she thought,
and wondered what he was thinking, for it had just
dawned upon her that she had been inconsistent, and
that was the reason he had guessed she cared for him.
'There's a lot about this whole business that I don't
understand,' he added slowly, his eyes never leaving
her face. 'You're either a damned good actress or
there's a grave mistake somewhere along the line.'

Lorna said nothing, merely looking at him for a
moment before turning away towards the door. He
had guessed that she wasn't as bad as he had believed,
but at the same time, with the lies told him by Gilbert,
he could not fathom her at all. She was furious with
herself for saying things that had revealed her hurt,
and also the fact that she cared for him. He now knew
that she had married him for love, and not for his
money, so all her vehement assertions to the contrary
had been in vain.

CHAPTER NINE

It was less than an hour later when, Lorna having procured her bracelet and then left Craig and returned to the castle alone, Craig told her that his grandmother had left all her money to charity.

She nodded, but he did not notice, so deep was his fury.

'Jeannie—to be denied everything,' he blazed, 'and all through you—damn you for coming here!'

'Through me?' Her chin lifted. 'How can you blame me? She had told you some time ago that she wanted to see you married to Jeannie.'

'True, but she'd not have changed her will if you hadn't come here——'

'You can't say that!' Her own anger was high despite her distress that Jeannie had lost everything. 'Mrs Lamond's a very strange woman—unpredictable. She could have decided to leave everything to charity even if I hadn't come up here and married you.'

His eyes were like points of steel boring into her. She noticed the wild pulsation of a nerve in his cheek, seeming to accentuate the little lines of crimson colour that so plainly denoted his inner fury.

'If you hadn't accepted her offer and come here, she'd have left the will as it was—— Oh, yes, she'd threatened several times to change her will, but she never would have done so simply because there wasn't anyone else to leave her money to. Then she saw you in hospital—a pretty girl who she obviously took to right from the start—and the idea of having another heir was born——'

'But you can't blame me for that!' broke in Lorna wrathfully. 'If she hadn't found me she'd probably have found someone else!'

'There wasn't any time,' he pointed out, gritting his teeth. 'She was near the end, and obviously she'd never have found anyone else! She used you as a lever to force my hand, believing I'd compel Jeannie to marry me rather than have you inherit what rightfully was ours. Jeannie was never told about the threat to change the will; Grandmother left it to me to work on her, but she was in ignorance of the fact that Jeannie's interest was elsewhere——'

'You know that Jeannie's engaged?' broke in Lorna, recalling that the girl had said she had never told her cousin anything about it.

'Yes, I know. Jeannie didn't tell me—I learned it elsewhere.'

'You said nothing to Jeannie—didn't warn her of what might happen?'

'Jeannie has a will of her own, a strong will. Nothing I could have said would have had any effect on Jeannie, so I didn't even trouble to let her know I'd discovered her secret. It's her own affair, not anybody else's.' His tone had less force and it did appear that he was realising the futility of brooding over his grandmother's action in leaving her vast fortune to charity. 'She obviously confided in you,' added Craig after a pause.

'Yes, she did. Jeannie and I got on very well together.'

'Because she had no idea what you'd come here

for—brought by Grandmother in order to be her legatee.' The scorn in his voice was reflected in his eyes and Lorna turned away, saying she was phoning the railway station to make sure there was a train for London at noon the following day.

'You really mean it about leaving me?' His face changed, the harshness dissolving into an expression she failed completely to understand. 'I asked you to stay until Grandmother dies.'

'Is there any special reason why you want me to stay?' she asked him curiously.

He hesitated, and when he eventually broke the silence he seemed almost persuasive, which was a dramatic change from the fury to which he had subjected her just a few moments ago.

'I asked you to share with me a little enjoyment——'

'Physical enjoyment?' She shook her head. 'I don't want you, Craig, and so I'm leaving you, tomorrow!' And with that she went from him, not seeing him again until she was getting ready for dinner, when without knocking he entered the bedroom and stood, just inside the door, his dark eyes roving her scantily-clad body.

'What do you want?' she demanded, blushing to the roots of her hair. 'Get out!'

'Be careful, Lorna,' was his softly-spoken warning as he slowly approached her. 'My wife doesn't speak to me like that.'

He came closer; she reached for a negligé, but he was there first, tossing it away on to the bed. She glanced down to the two dainty garments she wore and colour flooded into her face again. Craig reached her, his countenance a dark forbidding mask as he took hold of her round the waist and in spite of her struggles brought her close against his hard and angular frame.

Fear swelled within her as his brutal mouth, parted sensuously, came down and crushed hers. She would not be able to resist him, and she was terribly afraid of the results of intimacy between them. Already she could be carrying his child. . . .

'Leave me alone,' she pleaded hollowly when for a space he held her slightly away from him while keeping a firm hold on her arms. 'I don't want you. . . .'

'Liar! You want me as desperately as I want you,' he said hoarsely, his mouth against her ear. 'You've gone against all that's usual and let yourself care for me, haven't you?'

'No—no! I don't care for you——' The rest was ruthlessly stopped by his passionate kisses, by the warmth of his hands as they slid into the lacy briefs she wore.

'You do care, Lorna! And you want me! I said I'd compel you to admit it, and I'm now ordering you to admit it!'

'No ... I....' A spasm of sheer ecstasy ripped through her body as his hands continued to roam. She pressed so close that she felt the hard swelling of his passion against her stomach. 'I—oh, Craig, yes! I do want you!' It was no use to fight any more, to refuse to admit what her heart was crying out and her body was yearning for. 'Yes, I want you—I need you——' She gave her lips eagerly as he lifted her face with a little thrust of his hard chin.

'God, you're enough to make a man crazy!' He swung her up as he spoke, and carried her over to the bed, dropping her gently on to it and then standing over her as he undressed. Lorna quivered under his touch when presently he slid down beside her, and within minutes both were lost in a whirlpool of passion, carried to the heights of heaven as desire gave way to fulfilment.

Did he care? Lorna was repeating the question, as, much later, she was again getting ready for dinner, her husband having gone into the other room to dress. Undoubtedly his approach had been gentle, his lovemaking tender ... almost.

Almost but not quite, for there was a primitive quality about it now and then, as if he was suddenly aware that she did not deserve consideration ... because she was rotten?

She gave a deep sigh as she debated the result should she venture to tell him the truth. Would he believe her? She doubted it very much, because of what Gilbert had told him. And Lorna did have to admit that it looked very black against her. She *had* accepted the post with Mrs Lamond; Gilbert had told her that there would be very little work for her to do —although at the time she was so upset that she had not taken it in. But no doubt Craig had done so, when it was repeated to him by Gilbert.

She was a little late going down, so that Craig was before her. She halted by the open door of the elegant dining-room, broodingly watching him as he poured himself a drink. He was by the cocktail cabinet, superbly dressed in a light grey jacket and darker grey trousers. His shirt was gleaming white against a bronzed throat and wrists. She noticed the malely austere atmosphere that he created, with his features

carved in masculine perfection, his deep-set blue
eyes and uncompromising thrust of the jaw. His lips,
slightly apart, had a firm yet sensuous quality about
them which seemed to be accentuated by the strong,
even white teeth. Lorna's eyes wandered to the per-
fect silhouette of the hard lithe body that gave the
impression of latent male virility. Latent ... for how
long? That she aroused in him all that was allied to
primitive desire was more than evident even in his
glance as, suddenly aware of her presence, he looked
at her, his eyes glittering with a most odd expression.

'Come in,' he invited, his voice soft and low. 'What
are you standing there for?'

She shrugged and walked into the middle of the
room.

'I don't know,' she answered, flushing under his
intensive scrutiny.

'You're blushing, Lorna,' he said with a hint of
mockery. 'Another puzzling thing about you—that
you can blush.' No comment as she looked at the
empty glass on the cabinet—which had obviously
been put ready for whatever she might want in the
way of an aperitif. 'So the memory embarrasses you,
eh?'

'The memory?' she echoed, nonplussed.

'Of our recent—er—rather special interlude?'

Her colour deepened; she looked away, through
the window to the deer park and the tumbling burn
beyond.

'Can I have a drink?' she managed at length, making a supreme effort to regain her composure. 'I'd
like a dry vermouth, if you have it.'

'I think so.' But he made no move to pour her the
drink, going to her instead and drawing her into his
arms.

'Just what is it about you that's so different?' he said, bending to take her lips beneath his. 'You're transparent and mysterious at one and the same time.'

'That's an impossibility.'

'Not with you,' he argued. 'You're an enigma, for although there's plenty that's open about you there's also plenty that's hidden.'

Here was the opportunity of opening up and making an attempt to clear herself, an opportunity which it was impossible to let go by.

Lorna turned her face up, her eyes wide and appealing, her lips moving a little tremulously.

'Craig,' she began in a low, sincere tone, 'I'm going to——' She broke off as a quiet knock sounded on the door. It was opened and a maid appeared, glancing swiftly from Craig to his wife and back again.

'You're wanted, sir....' She backed, flicking a hand to indicate that he follow her, which he did, after giving her a frowning look.

'Excuse me, Lorna,' he apologised, 'I won't be long.'

Lorna watched him stride to the door and pass through it, leaving it ajar as he went out. What a strange way for a maid to act with her employer, mused Lorna, wondering at the tingling sensation that was fluttering along her spine. Curiosity getting the better of her, she went silently to the door, intending to open it and go out into the hall and make for the stairs, ostensibly to go to the bedroom for a handkerchief. But just as her hand came forth to bring the door inwards she heard a feminine voice say,

'But surely, Craig, there was some other way?'

'There was none!' Quiet the voice but wrathful.

'She was all set to make her will in her favour.'

'Oh, but, Craig—what about us?'

Lorna froze, wishing she could see what the girl was like. She sounded furious but she, like Craig, kept her voice low.

'There'll be a divorce——' Craig spoke brusquely, cutting the sentence as if it was not one that altogether pleased him. 'But——'

'It takes a long time—— I—I. . . .' the voice trailed away and Lorna knew the girl was choking with tears. 'This girl—she must be a hateful, avaricious person——'

'Come into the drawing-room,' interrupted Craig gently, 'and we can talk better there.'

So concerned he sounded, thought Lorna, remembering with painful intensity the way he usually spoke to her, with shortness and contempt.

They moved away and Lorna went over to the cabinet and poured herself a drink. She felt utterly flat, resolved to leave Craig within the next few days.

She was pale and silent when he returned, while he was grim-faced, and there was an antagonistic glint in his eyes as he looked at her.

'It's dinner time,' he said shortly, and went from the room again. She followed, leaving her drink, and they ate the meal in silence. Only when it was over and they were in the lounge did Lorna break the silence by saying, 'I heard you talking and know your visitor was the girl I mentioned—you were almost engaged to her?'

He shrugged; she wondered if what she saw in his eyes was unhappiness or regret. Perhaps it was a mixture of both.

'It doesn't matter,' he replied brusquely, taking up

his coffee cup and drinking from it. 'I'm married to you now.'

'But there's the divorce,' she reminded him, a hollow ring to her voice. 'Then you and she can go back to where you were.'

He looked at her curiously.

'You're very interested in my future,' he said.

'What's her name?' asked Lorna, ignoring this.

'Greta Scholfield. Her father owns the estate next to this.'

'On the other side of the burn? I've noticed the house when I was out walking. It's a huge mansion, and the grounds must be enormous.' She was talking for talking's sake, hiding her misery, her bitter disappointment at not being able to tell her husband those things she had been about to explain when she was interrupted by the arrival of his ex-girl-friend. Would it have made any difference if, having been given another five minutes, she had made her explanation to Craig? Lorna could not be sure, but in any case it was too late now; the moment was lost for ever.

He surprised her by suggesting a stroll in the grounds. She shook her head, saying she was tired.

'You seem depressed,' he said, 'rather than tired.'

'Depressed?' airily. 'What should I be depressed about?'

'The idea that I might be attracted to another woman,' was his candid reply, and she stared at him incredulously.

'Do you think I care!' she flashed, and was thrown a look of amused mockery for her trouble.

'Certainly you care. A woman in love is naturally a woman who's jealous of other women.'

'What a pompous, conceited ass you are!' she cried, getting up from her chair. 'I've no patience to talk to you!'

She was almost at the door when he said softly,

'Turn around, Lorna. . . .'

She shook her head dumbly, swiftly flicking a finger across her cheek.

'I'm going to—to my room——' He caught her without her even knowing he was there, and swung her around, tilting her head right back.

'You're crying,' he began, when she interrupted him, saying it was no such thing.

'I've got something in my eye!' she said finally, but her husband shook his head slowly from side to side. But he did not argue with her, kissing her instead, although at first he did meet with some resistance. However, he knew her well, was aware of how to excite her desires, create a physical awareness of him that she would find it impossible either to deny or control. He knew she was vibrantly conscious of him as a man, and that she would slowly—if reluctantly—cease her struggles and surrender to the persistence of his lips on hers. They were wide, burying her mouth in a full and sensuous blending of desire and forceful possession. She shuddered, ardour aroused to almost tempestuous heights as every tingling pulse and nerve responded to his demands and to the sheer mastery of his caressing, enticing hands on her breasts. His body curved in passionate desire towards hers, one hand straying down along her quivering spine to draw up her skirt. She twisted then, trying to escape, but he held her fast in a triumphant hold of hawser-like strength. His body was hard, like iron against her, his mouth seeking the tender curves of her throat before possessing her softly parted lips again. A spasm of ecstasy shuddered through her whole body and she was lost. Craig lifted her lightly and carried her from the room and up the stairs, her subconscious registering the fact that he might be seen by one of the servants, but her wild uncontrollable yearning cared nothing if he was. It was a moment of total abandonment, of forsaking all reality in favour of the glorious realm of bliss where thoughts and actions coalesced ... and two lovers became as one.

It was with a sense of total shock that Lorna awoke the following morning to find her husband no longer beside her. He had risen and left without a word. It was an action of complete indifference, rendering their lovemaking of the night before to less than nothing. Certainly it had made no impression on her husband; she was merely a convenience, an object with which to relieve his passions. Fury, white-hot and consuming filled her as she slid from between the sheets and stepped on to the floor. She would show him! She would be gone on his return from wherever he was.

With hasty movements she packed her cases, then washed and dressed and went down to the phone. There was a train, but when she phoned the taxi service she found to her disgust and frustration that their line was out of order.

A sigh of exasperation escaped her when suddenly she thought of Craig's car—the small one which was standing in the garage beside one of the larger ones. She could drive it!

Without any further hesitation she took up her

cases and scurried downstairs and out to the car. The cases were put into the boot, and only then did she think of the keys.

'Damn! Where would they be?'

A sound of footsteps on the gravel outside the garage made her shrink into the shadows at the back of the car. Katie! What could she be doing here? After only a moment's pause Lorna emerged from her place of concealment with the intention of questioning the girl, but Katie spoke first, staggering her listener by informing her that Mrs Lamond had come out of her coma.

'She's dazed, Miss—Mrs—but she's awake.' There was a deep frown furrowing the girl's narrow forehead and her lips were tight. 'She'll live to a hundred all right, the old. . . . Will you tell Mr Craig, and then come over? I've already phoned the doctor,' she ended, anticipating Lorna's question. 'I got his surgery, but he's out. However, they took a message and I think he won't be long in coming.'

As before Lorna's hesitation was momentary. It would appear, she reflected wryly, that she was again being kept from her intention by her former employer.

'I'll be right over, Katie,' she promised. 'Pehaps you would look around and find Mr Craig?'

'Yes, miss! Have you any idea where he might be?' Lorna shook her head.

'None at all,' she answered frankly. 'He'll be on the estate somewhere, of course.'

'He might have gone off by helicopter to the far moors,' suggested the girl, and Lorna had to agree.

'However,' she added, 'take a good look, and ask about. Some of the men might know where he is.'

There weren't many men about, Lorna noticed when she was passing through the castle grounds on her way to the little path leading from her husband's estate to that surrounding the Dower House.

The housekeeper was with Mrs Lamond, and another maid as well.

'How is she?' asked Lorna, moving softly from the door to the bed. The light was dim, the curtains drawn almost the full way across the windows, but for all that it was easy to see the old lady lying there, staring at the ceiling.

'She was just lying there and suddenly her eyes opened—so Katie said,' grunted the housekeeper brusquely. 'I thought the doctor said she'd never regain consciousness,' she added in a plaintive tone of voice. 'It looks as if he didn't know what he was talking about.'

Lorna, ignoring that, took Mrs Lamond's wrist between her fingers.

'You....' The parched lips moved twistedly and, it seemed, painfully. On the coverlet the gnarled hands grasped at nothing, then fell back as if they had as little strength as their owner. 'I w-want to—to talk—t-to you.' A pair of glazed watery eyes shifted almost imperceptibly. 'Tell her to go—it's you I w-want to—to see.'

Lorna turned, but already the housekeeper, her shoulders lifting in an aggrieved gesture, was at the door.

'What is it, Mrs Lamond?' enquired Lorna gently, her fingers still holding the woman's wrist. 'You shouldn't be talking, you know——'

'I hadn't any thought of giving it away to charity until you married my grandson.' Her voice was gaining strength and although it was very low at times every word came through to Lorna. 'I d-don't think you—you l-love him—and I'm sure he doesn't love you. Why don't you speak to me?'

'I will do, when you've finished. I'm glad you're recovering, Mrs Lamond,' Lorna added a trifle breathlessly. Would she rally sufficiently to make another will? She bent down to catch the next words for they were scarcely audible.

'I'm not going to recover, Lorna, but I must get strong enough to make another will. I'm leaving everything to you because I know without any doubt at all that you and Craig won't stay together. You'll leave him, won't you?'

Lorna was silent, aghast at the idea of the old woman making another will and again cutting out the rightful heirs.

'You can't leave it to me,' she began, 'as I'm not one of the family.'

'Not one of the family? So you *are* intending to leave him, then?' Despite her weakness, and the frailty of her sight now, she was able to add with confidence as she stared into Lorna's eyes, 'You're thinking of leaving him even now, because you know why he married you—a scoundrelly trick, wasn't it?'

'You can't leave me your money, Mrs Lamond,' said Lorna, ignoring her words. 'It belongs to Craig and Jeannie....' Her voice trailed, because Mrs Lamond had not heard; she was drifting away into oblivion again.

Releasing her hand, Lorna straightened the bed covers and moved over to the window, pulling aside the curtains and staring out. There was no sign either of Craig or of Katie, but into her vision there ap-

peared the figure of a woman, slim, swaying grace-
fully from the hips. She had entered the grounds by
the path leading from the castle and was looking towards the house as if looking for someone.

Lorna's nerves caught; she knew instinctively that
this woman was none other than the one who had
called last evening, the one Craig might have married
had he not married her, Lorna.

There was a ring at the bell, a sound of voices in
the hall as the housekeeper and the woman spoke to
one another.

'She's in the bedroom—this room here. You know,
though, where Mrs Lamond sleeps.'

'Can I go in?'

'I'll see.'

Lorna glanced at the door as the woman appeared.

'Miss Scholfield to see——' She stopped. 'She's
gone again?'

'Yes, I'm afraid so.' She looked beyond her to the
hall. 'Someone came to see her?'

'Yes. I'll tell her that——'

'It doesn't matter,' broke in the girl, coming to the
door and looking in, at Lorna, without even as much
as a glance at the bed. 'You can go,' imperiously as
she stepped aside to allow the housekeeper to pass.

'So your Craig's wife!' The girl walked in, her face,
pure-textured as alabaster, was hard and set, with
tight lips and eyes that looked like blue glass, and as
brittle. 'The gossip's rife about you,' she rasped. 'You
ingratiated yourself with this old woman so that you
could get your hands on her money, robbing both
Jeannie and Craig!' She was working herself up into
a temper and although her words had aroused a
similar fury within Lorna she did at least manage to

hold it effectively in check, her voice being coldly composed as she replied,

'Yes, I'm Craig's wife. He married me to serve his own purpose, as you know, since he obviously told you last evening——'

'He did!' snapped the girl, rudely breaking into what Lorna was saying. 'I returned unexpectedly from abroad—to find this happening!' She swung a hand disgustedly. 'To find you married to the man who loves me! He's been forced into it by an unscrupulous woman's scheming! But there'll be a divorce—you know that, don't you?'

Lorna nodded, pale to the lips.

'Yes, I know.'

'And then he'll marry me, just as he intended before you came on the scene to fawn and toady to this old hag, just to get your——'

'So there's to be a divorce?' It was Mrs Lamond who spoke, a sigh on her lips. 'That's what I wanted to hear, although, Lorna, I did say I knew that you and Craig would part company. A divorce.... It only strengthens my decision to leave everything to you, Lorna. I'm so glad you told me there was to be a divorce.'

'I didn't say it,' cried Lorna, 'it was her!'

'What's this all about?' queried the other girl, nonplussed. 'I thought she was unconscious.'

'No, my girl, I'm not unconscious! I heard everything you said and you're the last one I'd want my grandson to marry! Get out of my bedroom, girl— get out!'

She went, with a vicious glance in Lorna's direction as she passed her.

'I'm glad you said there's to be a divorce, Lorna.

If I leave you everything then I've really got my revenge on Craig, simply because when you go you'll take my money with you.'

'Mrs Lamond,' began Lorna desperately, 'I——'

'I feel so ill, Lorna,' gasped the old woman. 'Give me some tablets.'

'I think we ought to wait until the doctor comes.'

'No ... give them to me and then get my solicitor on the phone. Tell him to come at once—at once, Lorna, because there isn't much time....'

'But I....' Lorna's voice trailed as an idea flashed like a sudden dart of light and hope into her mind. She could let Mrs Lamond leave the money to her and then make it over by deed of gift to Jeannie and Craig! So simple! Yes, there was need for haste, she owned, glancing at Mrs Lamond's heaving chest, her blue lips and sunken eyes. 'Yes, Mrs Lamond,' she said eagerly. 'I'll get your solicitor and have him make me your heir!'

'That's what you want?' in some surprise and yet with a deep-throated sigh of satisfaction. 'You want to have my fortune left to you?'

'Yes, Mrs Lamond, I do!'

'Good girl! Then act with haste, child, because there's very little time left to me. Phone from my boudoir at once.'

Lorna needed no extra bidding as she ran to the door. She went through it, her eyes catching sight of something fluttering round the corner of the hall. She frowned. It had looked like material blown in the wind.... Must be mistaken, she thought as she went swiftly to Mrs Lamond's boudoir. Within seconds she had dialled the number and was listening for the voice at the other end of the line.

'Come quickly,' she urged. 'Mrs Lamond's wanting to alter her will——'

'What, again?'

'Yes, she—— Oh, please hurry! There's very little time!' She knew she sounded distressed, speaking in an almost frenzied tone of voice. 'She wants you now, at once!'

CHAPTER TEN

KATIE returned a short while later with the information that Craig could not be found and it was believed that he had gone with his factor, in the jeep, to hunt for a fox that had taken two newly-born lambs.

'He could be all day, then,' said Lorna with a sigh. She had hoped he would arrive before the lawyer so that she could explain what was in her mind regarding his grandmother's will.

The doctor arrived about the same time as the lawyer but did not stay more than a few minutes, saying there was nothing he could do; Mrs Lamond had done the unexpected and come out of the coma and there was no knowing how long she would live now.

'Send for me when you notice a change,' he told Lorna, and made his departure just as the lawyer was unfastening his briefcase. The will was drawn up, with the lawyer glancing at Lorna as he heard the instructions. Lorna went out, feeling embarrassed and desiring nothing except the opportunity of employing him herself, to make out the two deeds of gift. But she could not do that until Mrs Lamond's death simply because she would not inherit before then.

'She'll probably change it again when the fancy takes her,' said the lawyer derisively as he made to leave, along with the office clerk he had brought along as second witness to Mrs Lamond's signature. 'It was incredible that she could manage to write so legibly, with her hand trembling like that and the paper on a pad right in front of her face.'

'I'm satisfied now,' sighed the old lady, when Lorna re-entered the room, 'I can die in peace.'

Lorna could not help but look contemptuously at her, finding no pity in her heart even now, when death was so close.

She left soon after the lawyer, arriving back just a few minutes before her husband who, walking into the drawing-room where she was seated, her eyes staring, her mind dwelling on all that had taken place, said in guttural, vibrant tones,

'Where are you going? Why are your suitcases in the car?'

'My——?' Lorna had forgotten all about them during the momentous events which had taken place, and even on her arrival back at the castle the matter had not entered her consciousness. She stammered an explanation—that she had intended leaving him that day but Katie had come over for her.

'Katie?' he repeated, diverted. 'What did she want you for?'

'It was your grandmother—she came out of the coma. Katie went to find you, but——'

'Grandmother came out of her coma?' echoed Craig disbelievingly. 'What is the woman made of?'

'She wanted to. . . .' Lorna's voice came slowly to a stop as Greta Scholfield approached the room from across the lawn.

Both Lorna and Craig watched her, taking smooth and confident steps, covering the small distance quickly and arriving at the french window just as Craig was opening it.

'Craig—oh, you're back! I've been wandering

about, looking for you!' She glanced at Lorna with an expression of dark venom. 'I must speak to you alone, Craig—at once!'

Lorna backed away, then turned, leaving the room as swiftly as the girl had entered it. She appeared to be in great distress, mused Lorna, little knowing what the girl was at this moment relating to Craig.

'She was so eager to get the solicitor, Craig!' These added words were spoken so loudly that Lorna did manage to catch them as she walked along the hall. She stopped, her heart pounding against her ribs. 'I heard her say she wanted your grandmother to make a new will in her favour—she was begging her to do so, Craig—and there was such a nauseating urgency about her as she ran out to phone the lawyer. She didn't see me because I ran round the corner of the hall as she came from the bedroom, but I was there, even when she phoned, and she was frantic to get the man here so that the will could be changed in her favour. Craig,' cried the girl in tones of sheer frustration, 'she's got everything that's yours and Jeannie's!'

'My God, what sort of a vile snake is she? I'd strangle her if I thought I could get away with it— strangle her slowly so that she'd scream for mercy! Where is she? I'll take a riding-crop to her if....' His voice faded as Lorna, her face drained of all colour, moved on legs that felt like jelly, moved silently to the door and passed just as silently through it.

She raced for the car, transferring her cases into the big one where, she had previously noticed, the key was in the ignition. It was a huge car, but she felt she could manage it, and she did, breathing normally only when she was on the road, running smoothly on towards the town.

The railway station was her destination and to her immense relief there was a train actually alongside the platform. It was going only to Edinburgh, but she could lose herself there for the few hours until the night train for London came in. Craig would brand her a thief, but tomorrow he would be informed that his car had been left abandoned at the station.

Her aunt came to the door, standing with it in her hand as she stared perplexedly at her niece.

'Can't I come in?' Lorna had paid the taxi and she was on the step beside her two suitcases.

'Of c-course, dear—but what's wrong? Have you decided to give up your job?' Consternation on her face and in her voice; bitterly Lorna looked at her before picking up her cases and stepping into the long narrow hall of the Victorian house to which she had come after the tragic deaths of her parents.

'I won't stay long,' she faltered, turning to her aunt as she closed the door. 'I'll explain it all to you in a minute.'

Half an hour later Lorna, having carefully omitted a great deal of the full story, had given her aunt a fairly feasible explanation of why she had left her employment. She had merely said that from the first she had sensed a mystery, and felt that her employer had intended using her for some purpose known both to herself and her grandson. Lorna had felt that matters were getting worse, and that they would become still worse—which they would have done, she thought grimly, had she stayed and come in for the full force of her husband's wrath. When she had finished her aunt sighed and then, rather hesitantly, asked if Lorna could ever become interested in Gilbert again.

Lorna's eyes flickered as she recalled the idea she had had that things had gone wrong between Gilbert and Susan.

'Why do you ask, Aunt Mary?' she queried.

'He's free again, Lorna. The affair ended almost as soon as it had begun. Susan did to him what he'd done to you: she met someone else. I believe he tried desperately to persuade her to give this man up, but she obviously had no intention of doing so because, only three weeks later, the announcement of her engagement was made public.'

'So he got his deserts. . . .' Did she feel any satisfaction at his heartache? Not really . . . and yet, after the pain she herself had known at the time he threw her over, Lorna could not help but feel that he deserved all he'd received.

'Yes, he got his deserts, Lorna, but when I saw him I gained the impression that he wished he'd never thrown you over, that he still loved you, dear. He begged me to write to you—— Now when was it? Yes, only about a fortnight after you'd gone up to Scotland, and to tell you how he felt. But I said it was too soon; you were feeling far too bitter and it would be advisable for him to wait a while longer, to allow you to settle down, as it were.'

'I could never care for him again,' declared Lorna. 'I'd be unable to forget what he did to me.'

'I believe you would, in time.' A small pause ensued, but Lorna, remembering all Gilbert had done to her, apart from throwing her over, remained silent.

'Why don't you agree to meet him, Lorna, and then see how you feel?'

'It isn't any use,' returned Lorna, trying to keep the impatience from her voice. 'It's finished, Aunt.'

The older woman shook her head.

'I don't think you're being very rational about it, dear. Many couples part and then come together again. Why don't you phone him——' She was stopped by the decisive shake of her niece's head. 'Oh, very well,' she added, sighing. 'Just as you like, dear.'

Lorna looked at her; there was nothing in her expression to reveal whether or not she was wishing her niece had stayed away, up in Scotland.

'I won't stay here with you,' said Lorna after a moment, and with some difficulty, 'because I'm sure you and Uncle have got used to being on your own, and enjoy it. In any case, I'd feel better if I had my own flat. You know how it is,' she went on, assuming an apologetic manner, 'when you've been on your own, away from home? You feel you don't want to lose your new-found independence, if you know what I mean?' She watched her aunt's face closely, saw the relief that crossed it before saying, adopting an attitude of understanding,

'It's up to you, Lorna dear. You know we've never regretted taking you into our home; you've given us a great deal of pleasure. However, if you feel you want a place of your own, then neither your uncle nor I would dream of trying to stop you.'

It was with difficulty that Lorna suppressed the smile of grim bitterness that came to her lips as she listened to this. However, she had no wish to upset her aunt in any way and she merely said lightly,

'I'm so glad you understand, Aunt Mary—but I knew you would!'

When her uncle arrived from work explanations were made, this time by Lorna's aunt because Lorna was upstairs, in her old room, unpacking and making up the bed, which had been stripped and a dust sheet thrown over it. It had been a forlorn aspect that met Lorna's eyes as she stood on the familiar threshold, her suitcases in her hand. Empty, like her heart and her life. A shuddering sigh had escaped her before, with a light of resolution in her eyes, she had rallied and told herself that life was by no means finished for her. She was strong; she'd get over this in time.

She would feel much better in any case when she had got rid of the legacy left to her by Mrs Lamond.

It was only a week before she found a flat and moved in, taking all the things that were stored at her aunt's house—things bought for the home she had been going to make with Gilbert. Her aunt had given her some furniture and she had bought some more. The flat was cosy and bright by the time Lorna had finished, and this alone lifted her spirits immensely. The look of strain and pallor left her face; her hair became brighter.

'You look so different!' exclaimed her aunt when she called on her with a bunch of flowers she had thought to buy her. 'I think it's a wonderful idea for you to have your own place!'

Lorna said nothing, but went to the bright little kitchen to make some tea and toast. When she returned her aunt said tentatively,

'I happened to bump into Gilbert this morning in

town. Naturally I told him you were back——'

'Oh, I wish you hadn't! It's nothing to do with him, Aunt Mary!'

'Well, I'm sorry, then, but I didn't think you'd mind. After all, you could just have easily bumped into him as I did.'

'Yes, you're quite right. I could.'

'And at the hospital ... they'll soon know you're back in the district.'

'I don't know about that. I'm going to work in London itself—in the city, I mean.'

'You have a post?'

Lorna shook her head.

'Not yet, but I'm sure I can get something.'

'You've enough to manage on, for the present, I mean?'

'Yes, thank you, Aunt. I saved a good deal of money in a very short time. Mrs Lamond was exceedingly generous,' she added on a distinct note of bitterness which could not possibly escape her aunt but upon which she decided not to comment.

'I must be off,' her aunt was saying an hour later. 'You're sure you don't want to see Gilbert?'

Lorna looked directly at her and said,

'Aunt Mary, you don't know the half of the story. Gilbert played me a hateful trick before I went up to Scotland.'

On the point of leaving, her aunt paused.

'In what way, Lorna?'

A slight hesitation and then,

'It doesn't matter any more. It's enough that you know I have other things against him than that he jilted me.'

*

After her aunt's departure Lorna sat down and thought about all that had happened to her during the past few months. She could not forget Gilbert's infamy and yet, strangely, she was taking it philosophically, as one of those occurrences in life that are out of one's control. It was fated that she should be played this hateful trick by the man she had at that time loved, and what was done was done and nothing to be gained by dwelling on it.

And yet, she was thinking only seconds later, how could one help dwelling on it when it had affected one's life the way it had hers? She had lost Craig, earned only his bitter contempt at first and his hatred later. None of it would have happened had not Gilbert in his eagerness to rid himself of her, told detestable and inexcusable lies about her to Craig, lies that fitted so well with her unconscious acceptance of the post up in Scotland that Craig could scarcely be blamed for his attitude towards her. She was all bad—— All ...? He had begun to doubt it as he got to know her; he had come almost to the point where he would have listened to her side of the story, and she had been ready to tell it to him. Fate had intervened in the form of the girl who, quite understandably, had a grudge against Lorna, and so the story had never been told and instead Lorna had fled in fear from her husband's fury.

Her thoughts switched and she was dwelling with brooding darkness on that last will made by Mrs Lamond. Lorna's first act upon arriving back at her aunt's flat was to write to the lawyer asking to be informed immediately the old woman died.

'If she doesn't alter her will again,' she had added, 'then please prepare two deeds of gift, as I intend to

make half the money over to Miss MacFarlane and
the other half to my husband, Craig Lamond.'

She had wondered, since then, if the lawyer would
tell Craig of her intention, then had realised that he
would never dream of telling anyone else of the
wishes of a client of his. Well, Craig would know immediately his grandmother died, and perhaps his
opinion of her would then change. But there was no
future for them; of that she felt very sure. Craig
would realise, as she did, that too much had passed
between them that was unpleasant; the gulf was far
too wide for them to scale.

And yet *was* it too wide for them to scale? If it
should transpire that Craig cared....

Only the future could bring an answer. If Craig
wanted her he would learn from the lawyer where she
was.

Three days later she answered a ring at the door and
found herself looking into the cool, unsmiling face
of her ex-fiancé.

'What do you want?' she frowned, beginning to
close the door and then changing her mind as she
realised there was no need for such rudeness.

'Lorna,' said Gilbert unsteadily, 'I must talk to
you. I saw your aunt——'

'I told her I didn't want to see you,' she interrupted
shortly. 'You and I have nothing to talk about, Gilbert.'

He frowned at her.

'You're not as heartless as you're trying to make
out, Lorna. Please ask me in.'

She opened the door wider, an automatic action
born of the deep dejection she saw in his eyes. He had

lost everything through his behaviour in jilting her, and yet now that she saw him again she realised she did not hate him as much as she had believed she did. It was rather indifference she felt, and she was at the same time thankful she had not married him, for it would never have worked out, just as he himself had stated at the time.

'Come in, then,' she invited, closing the door after him.

He sat down and glanced around the pretty little room with its nylon drapes that looked like velvet, rich crimson and luxurious. The carpet was fitted, the windowsill bright with potted flowering plants.

'It's nice here—— You're a homemaker, Lorna.'

'I like it,' she returned coolly. 'It's big enough for me, and it's comfortable.'

'It certainly is. Er—have you a job yet?'

'Not yet.'

'But you'll be getting one, I suppose?'

'I shall have to, won't I——?' she stopped, glancing swiftly at him. 'We're talking for talking's sake, Gilbert. I think you ought to go.'

'No!' Distress looked out from his eyes. 'Lorna, I made a ghastly mistake. It was you I loved all the time! The affair with Susan was breaking up even before you went away——'

'That day, in the café when we were saying good-bye, you knew then, didn't you? But you still held on to the hope that Susan wouldn't throw you over as you threw me——'

'I admit it was troubling me that day, and I admit I was desperate for her not to give me up. But since then I've realised quite definitely that it's you I love, and if you could bring yourself to forgive me, you would never regret it, Lorna. I'd do everything in my power to make it up to you!'

Her eyes never left his face as he spoke and she knew without any doubt at all that he was sincerely sorry that he had given her up. She recalled all the lies he had told about her, his infamous conduct, his shirking of the responsibility of the break-up, saying he could not face the gossip at the hospital. She opened her mouth to remind him of it all, then closed it again, admitting that any recriminations were unprofitable. What he had done did not matter any more; it hurt only in that she had lost Craig through it. Or had she...? There was a faint hope in her heart that once her husband learned of her intention of giving up all right to the inheritance, he would come to her and ask her to go back and share his life and his home. It was only a vague hope, a faint flicker of light in a deep dark valley of despair, but it was there, and Craig alone could make it light up the whole of her life ... or extinguish it for ever.

'It isn't any use, Gilbert,' she said at last, shaking her head. 'I don't want you....' She paused, half inclined to tell him she was married, but then realised that should he bump into her aunt again he would be bound to mention it, and she felt—at present anyway —that she did not want her aunt and uncle to know she was married. 'Please go. I'd rather not prolong this conversation. It's not making any sense, is it?'

She saw his face darken with sudden anger and a frown of bewilderment knit her brow.

'You haven't given me a chance!' he said harshly. 'Why can't you say you'll consider, try to forgive me? I've been honest about Susan, but I've been honest as well about my feelings for you. I love you, Lorna! I mean it! I love you!'

Totally unaffected, she spread her hands and indicated the door.

'It's best for us both that you leave,' she advised. 'Because otherwise we shall be quarrelling.'

He rose, much to her relief, and she showed him to the door, opening it wide to reveal the charming little porchway with its flowers in boxes and on a shelf running at right angles to the outer door, which was also open, as Gilbert had not closed it when he came into the porch. Lorna never locked it because the bell was on the inner door.

'Goodbye,' she said calmly. 'You'll find someone else eventually.'

'Never! It's you I want!' His voice sounded almost vicious—so unlike the old Gilbert she had known, she thought. But then he was under the influence of a very strong emotional stress; this was obvious by the convulsive twisting of his mouth and the strange glitter in his eyes.

'You think that now,' she told him. 'But one day all this will pass and——' She broke off on a strangled little exclamation as, taking her completely by surprise, Gilbert caught her in his arms and crushed her protesting body against his. She sensed the brutality of the lips as he bent his head and she began to struggle violently, twisting about in an attempt to free herself from his hold.

'Stop struggling, Lorna!' he rasped, obviously so carried away by emotion that he scarcely knew what he was doing. 'Kiss me, damn you! You loved me once and could again if only you'd let bygones be bygones! Stop struggling, I say——' He got no further. Lorna, her senses reeling by this time, was vaguely aware of another presence, of being rescued as Gilbert, grasped by his coat collar as a lean brown

hand shot out, went staggering back into the sitting-
room and she heard the crash of a flower vase falling
as his head hit the table.

'Craig——!' she began, but was thrust uncere-
moniously aside as Craig strode purposefully towards
the man who was getting unsteadily to his feet.

'What the hell are you doing making love to my
wife!' snarled Craig, grasping him by the lapels of his
coat and jerking him forward. Lorna, having managed to follow on legs that felt as if the bones within
them had melted, winced as she realised that Gilbert's
tongue had been caught between his teeth.

'Your ... wife?' murmured Gilbert when he could
speak. 'Lorna ... married to you?' His eyes seemed
glazed as they moved to her face. Craig flung him
back viciously and he went over the arm of the
couch on to the seat itself.

'Leave him alone, Craig,' faltered Lorna, fearing,
by her husband's savage expression, that he would
pick Gilbert up again and fetch him a crashing blow
with his fist. 'I—he——'

'Get out!' thundered Craig, again ignoring his
wife.

Gilbert rose but stood where he was, his handsome
face twisted as if in pain as he looked at Lorna and
then at Craig.

'She's not married to you, Craig,' he said vehe-
mently. 'You—you didn't even like her.'

Craig's eyes, narrowed and threatening, settled on
him for a moment before he said,

'I advise you to get out, Gilbert. You and I have
nothing to say to one another because the way I feel
at this moment, it's action I'm itching for, not words.'
The threat in his voice was made more dangerous by

the guttural tone and by the slow closing of his fists on which Lorna's fascinated eyes were fixed. That Craig was on her side was plain to her, but her mind was so chaotic, disturbed by the dramatic events of the past few moments, that she scarcely assimilated the fact that there might be a happy ending for her.

'You're not married to him, are you, Lorna?' persisted Gilbert, looking at her. 'If you were you wouldn't be here, making a home for yourself. Also, you never mentioned anything about marriage to your aunt——'

'Gilbert,' she interrupted just as her husband opened his mouth to do so, 'please go. I *am* married to Craig——'

'No! I don't believe either of you!' stormed Gilbert wildly. 'There's some stupid reason why you're both lying——' He got no further as, his patience exhausted, Craig reached out to grasp him by the collar. Lorna managed to step between them, turning imploringly to Craig.

'Let him go peacefully, Craig. I'm not having a fight here, in my home.' For the first time he gave her his attention, and as his stare stretched and his expression changed she gave an involuntary little gasp that was akin to a sigh of sheer, undiluted happiness, for what she saw there, in those dark and deep-set eyes, was more than enough to dissolve all doubt and despair and instead to send her spirits soaring to the heights.

Gilbert hesitated only a mere few seconds before moving slowly to the door. It had barely closed behind him when Craig, opening wide his arms, ordered sharply,

'Come here, Lorna!'

Doubt touched her heart at his tone, but she went obediently towards him.

'Craig ... you came because of the—the will?'

The dark eyes took on a censorious quality as he replied,

'Yes, that's why I'm here—but, girl, why didn't you tell me the truth when I tried to draw you out? On several occasions I gave you an opening to explain. I knew you weren't all bad and I said so——'

'The time wasn't right at first,' she broke in in an attempt to vindicate herself. 'And on that last occasion——' She stopped, shuddering, and it was some seconds before she could manage to tell him that she had overheard him telling Greta that he would take a whip to her. 'I was afraid of you,' she whispered, and at the real fear in her voice her husband brought her close within his protective arms and, bending his head, kissed her tenderly on the lips.

And for a while there was no need for words between them as they clung to each other in the silence, their lips locked together, their bodies melded as if they were one.

Eventually, however, they did talk, sitting close together on the settee, and it was exactly as Lorna had dared to hope: the result of her action in giving away the fortune had convinced her husband that there was a great deal he did not know.

'Grandmother did rally again before she died,' he eventually told Lorna, 'and she was rambling on about the will, saying she'd made a mistake and ought not to have made you her legatee because, on thinking about it, she was of the opinion that you were too conscientious to accept that money.'

'She was thinking about the buttons I returned,'

commented Lorna when he paused. 'And my refusal of the other gifts of the family jewels she offered me——' Too late she stopped, blushing with embarrassment as it was borne in on her that this was not something she ought to be revealing, since it seemed rather in the nature of illustrating her honesty. But Craig's eyes were lit only with tenderness as he said,

'So you refused other gifts, did you?'

She nodded.

'I took the buttons, Craig, because she threatened to keep me with her until I had accepted them. It was the night you'd invited me to dinner and I was so eager not to be late that I took them, intending to return them the following day, which I did.'

He was nodding, recalling that she had been late that night, her excuse being the truthful one that Mrs Lamond had kept her.

'I've been a brute to you,' he declared regretfully, and yet the next moment it was only sternness that edged his voice. 'But for all that I ought to beat you thoroughly for allowing me to continue harbouring animosity against you.' His arms were about her and he gave her a little shake. 'You need only to have spoken and I'd have listened, because I was falling in love with you: I adore you,' he said, and there was unbelievable tenderness in his voice now, 'but I'm angry with you as well!'

'You were telling me about your grandmother rambling on about the will,' interposed Lorna hastily, wanting only to veer his thoughts away from such things as anger. 'She regretted making me her beneficiary, you said.'

'It must have suddenly come to her that your eagerness to have the will changed was feigned, a ruse to get her to withdraw it from charity and give it to you. She realised what your intention was: to put everything right by passing the money over to Jeannie and me. Well,' he added, and there was no mistaking the satisfaction in his voice, 'she didn't have time to send even yet again for her lawyer. She died before she had time to undo what she knew she had made a mistake in doing, which was, of course, leaving her money to you.'

'Have you seen Jeannie?' she asked, snuggling close against his shoulder.

'Yes. She knows what you're intending doing and is very grateful—not for herself, I think, but for her mother, who has always blamed herself, in a way, for Jeannie's being deprived.'

'Jeannie isn't deprived,' argued Lorna, leaning away and looking into her husband's eyes. 'No one who has love is deprived, Craig. They have everything that's precious. Don't you agree, darling?'

'Yes, my dearest wife,' responded Craig huskily as he drew her close again, 'anyone who has love has everything that's precious!'

The Mills & Boon Rose is the Rose of Romance

Look for the Mills & Boon Rose next month

CHANCE MEETING *by Kay Thorpe*
Lee Brent was socially and financially right out of Sharon's
league, and the last thing she wanted was to discover why he
had really married her . . .

PRISONER IN PARADISE *by Marjorie Lewty*
Stranded in Mexico, Sara's rescuer was the formidable Jason
Knight, who made no secret of his low opinion of her.

SET THE STARS ON FIRE *by Sally Wentworth*
When actress Lori West joined a film company in Rhodes, she
was aware of hostility from everyone there — in particular
from the director, Lewis Brent.

HALF A WORLD AWAY *by Gloria Bevan*
On a trip to New Zealand, Nicola met and fell in love with
Keith Lorimer, but he didn't seem to feel anything but
friendship for her . . .

YESTERDAY'S SCARS *by Carole Mortimer*
Because of what had once passed between Hazel and her stern
cousin-guardian Rafe Savage, she found how he was now bitter and
unforgiving, scarred in more than body . . .

CAROLINE'S WATERLOO *by Betty Neels*
Could Caroline settle for a marriage to the imposing Professor
Radinck Thoe van Erckelens when it was clear that there was
to be no romance involved?

THE LEO MAN *by Rebecca Stratton*
James Fraser was a typical Leo man, thought Rowan — bossy!
But she found herself rapidly revising her opinion.

A RING FOR A FORTUNE *by Lilian Peake*
Sloan Lancaster agreed to marry Jasmine so that she could
inherit her grandfather's fortune, although Sloan made no
pretence of feeling anything for her but contempt . . .

MISS HIGH AND MIGHTY *by Margaret Rome*
How could Jade convince her husband, the lordly Dom Diego
da Luz Pereira da Silves, that he was wrong to accuse her of
marrying him for his money?

THE BUTTERFLY AND THE BARON *by Margaret Way*
Renee Dalton was a rich society butterfly, and the forceful,
down-to-earth Nick Garbutt had no opinion of her at all.

If you have difficulty in obtaining any of these books from
your local paperback retailer, write to:

Mills & Boon Reader Service
P.O. Box 236, Thornton Road, Croydon, Surrey, CR9 3RU.

Available July 1980